The SECRET HORSES of BRIAR HILL

The SECRET HORSES of BRIAR HILL

MEGAN SHEPHERD

Illustrated by DAN BURGESS

DELACORTE PRESS

Text copyright © 2016 by Megan Shepherd
Jacket art and interior illustrations copyright © 2016 by Dan Burgess

All rights reserved. Published in the United States by Delacorte Press, an imprint of Random House Children's Books, a division of Penguin Random House LLC, New York.

Delacorte Press is a registered trademark and the colophon is a trademark of Penguin Random House LLC.

Visit us on the Web! randomhousekids.com

Educators and librarians, for a variety of teaching tools, visit us at RHTeachersLibrarians.com

Library of Congress Cataloging-in-Publication Data
Names: Shepherd, Megan, author. | Burgess, Dan, illustrator.
Title: The secret horses of Briar Hill / Megan Shepherd ; illustrated by Dan Burgess.
Description: First edition. | New York : Delacorte Books for Young Readers, 2016. |
Summary: "A girl living in a children's hospital during WWII discovers that a winged horse has entered her world and needs her help" —Provided by publisher.
Identifiers: LCCN 2015044878 (print) | LCCN 2016021671 (ebook) |
ISBN 978-1-101-93975-8 (hardback) | ISBN 978-1-101-93977-2 (glb) |
ISBN 978-1-101-93976-5 (ebk)
Subjects: | CYAC: Hospitals—Fiction. | Sick—Fiction. | Horses—Fiction. |
Death—Fiction. | World War, 1939–1945—Fiction. |
BISAC: JUVENILE FICTION / Animals / Horses. | JUVENILE FICTION /
Social Issues / Death & Dying. | JUVENILE FICTION / Historical / Holocaust.
Classification: LCC PZ7.S54374 Se 2016 (print) | LCC PZ7.S54374 (ebook) |
DDC [Fic]—dc23

The text of this book is set in 12.7-point Centaur.
Interior design by Heather Kelly

Printed in the United States of America
10 9 8 7 6 5 4 3 2 1
First Edition

Random House Children's Books supports the
First Amendment and celebrates the right to read.

In memory of my grandfather

Before the war, the hospital wasn't a hospital at all.
It was the house of a beautiful, rich princess.

1

I HAVE A SECRET.

I won't tell Benny and the other boys. They are like dogs in the night, snarling at anything that moves, chasing cats along country roads just for the thrill of watching them run. I won't tell Anna, either, even though she is nice to me and shares her colored pencils, even the turquoise one that is her favorite because it reminds her of the sea near her home. Sister Constance tells me that Anna could die soon, and I should be *careful* and *quiet* around her. Around Anna I have to tiptoe, I have to pretend that everything is okay, I have to keep secrets to myself.

But I'll tell you.

This is my secret: there are winged horses that live in the mirrors of Briar Hill hospital.

2

ANNA IS ASLEEP AGAIN.

I lie on the foot of her bed so that I won't wake her, drawing on the backs of the war pamphlets Sister Constance keeps in a stack by the fireplace for the grounds-keeper, Thomas, to use as kindling for the wood he has chopped. There is a gilded mirror above Anna's chest of drawers. It reflects the mirror-me. The mirror-Anna, snoring. The mirror-room, with its wool blankets strung over the window to hide our lights from outside at night. And, standing in the mirror-doorway, is a winged horse that isn't in Anna's room at all. The mirror-horse is nosing through the half-finished cup of tea that Anna left on her bedside table. He has a soft gray muzzle that is beaded with droplets of tea, and quicksilver hooves, and snow-white wings folded tightly. It's hard to capture with a pencil how horse ears are both round and pointy at the same time.

Benny comes in and sneers at my drawing. His thin red hair, combed back with a wide part down the middle, and his sharp hungry eyes make me think of the rawboned hunting dogs that are always looking for something to make a meal of.

"Horses don't have horns," he says.

"Those are its ears."

"They don't have wings, either."

My hand tightens around the pencil. "Some of them do."

Benny rolls his eyes. "Sure, and Bog is actually a dragon, even though he looks like a flea-bitten old collie."

Anna wakes, then, and tells Benny to leave, and he does because Anna is the oldest and because she asks him nicely.

"Come here, Emmaline," Anna says, "and show me what you've drawn."

She wraps her cardigan around my shoulders as I crawl into bed next to her, and gives me a tight squeeze, as snug as if I were home. "What lovely creatures," she says as she inspects my drawing. "You've such an imagination."

She smiles warmly, but she smells sour, like milk left outside too long. Her face is very pale, except for the places where it is so red it looks chapped, even though it has been many weeks since she has been outside.

I glance at the mirror.

The winged horse has grown bored with Anna's tea and is backing out of the mirror-room, bumping his rump against the tight angles of the mirror-hallway. I cover my mouth to keep from giggling. Anna can't see the winged horses in the mirrors.

No one can—only me.

It was late summer when I first arrived at Briar Hill. Sister Constance took me straight to her office and removed the identification tag pinned to my coat. While she made notations in a ledger, I tried to smooth my tufts of hair in the mirror above her desk. Then, completely out of nowhere, *completely without warning*, a winged horse clomped straight through the mirror-doorway, prim as anything, tail held high, as though Sister Constance's office were the exact place he was looking for.

"A horse!" I yelled, pointing at the mirror. He was nosing around Sister Constance's desk. "With wings! And it's eating your ruler!"

Sister Constance gave me a look like I'd said Winston Churchill was holding a pink parasol while riding an elephant across occupied France.

"There!" I pointed to the mirror again. "Now it's gotten your pencil!"

She turned to the mirror.

She looked back at me.

She called for the doctor.

Dr. Turner came and felt my forehead, and they spoke quietly to each other by the windows while I tapped my finger against the mirror again and again and again like I used to do with the live fish in the tanks at the fishmonger's. The horse didn't turn. He didn't glance at me at all. He just leaned against the blackboard and fell asleep, while outside Sister Constance's door, I heard the other children whispering about me.

"Emmaline?" Anna asks. "What are you giggling about?"

I look away from the winged horse with tea on his muzzle. Anna coughs, pressing her hankie to her mouth. Something stirs in my lungs too, still and thick as swamp water. It makes me think of the expression Mama uses when Papa teases me for being sullen. She'll look up from her book with a smile and say, *Leave her be, Bill. There's mystery in the quiet ones. Still waters run deep.*

And this—this liquid, this sickness—there is nothing in the world that could run deeper.

"Emmaline?" Anna squeezes my shoulder.

"It's nothing."

Anna hands me back my drawing. With my thick pink eraser, I rub away the ears that I've drawn wrong.

"You like horses, don't you?" she asks. Even with her cough, her voice is gentle.

I blow away the bits of crumbled eraser. I start to re-draw the ear. Benny is daft if he thinks it looks like a horn.

"We had workhorses at the bakery," I say, and add a little tuft of hair coming from its ear. "A big gelding and two bay mares. Spice, Nutmeg, and Ginger. They were beautiful. They had sandy brown hair and dark manes. They wouldn't ever come when the bakery boys called to them, but they never ran away from me."

"I guess horses can tell a lot about people," Anna says.

I look up at her. Her eyebrows are knit together. It is the same look that Sister Constance gets when she goes into the kitchen pantry to take inventory of the dusty cans of ham. There are fewer and fewer of them each week.

"You must miss them terribly," Anna adds, reaching out to brush back my hair. "I'm sure once you go home they'll come right up to their stall doors, begging for an apple." She starts coughing again, but pretends it's just a tickle, and takes a sip of cold tea. "You can tell them stories about these flying horses in your drawings. Perhaps, long ago, they were cousins."

I stop drawing.

Anna is looking toward the window, as though something has caught her eye. When Dr. Turner told her she couldn't leave the bed again, the Sisters pinned back a corner of the hanging wool blanket so that she could have some fresh air. In the hand mirror propped by her bedside table, there's a flicker of movement. A winged horse is passing by in the mirror-world outside. I can catch only a glimpse of him in the reflected window. He stretches his wings like

"You like horses, don't you?" she asks.

he's been asleep all morning. Anna's eyes jerk toward the mirror. Her eyebrows knit together again, more curiously this time.

Has she seen it?

Has she seen the winged horse?

After that first day in Sister Constance's office, I haven't spoken of the winged horses again—except secretly, just a little, to Anna. Everyone else snickers at me behind my back, but Anna would never do that.

And for a moment, as she studies the mirror, I think she might see the horse too.

But then she sighs, and adjusts the barrette in her hair, and flips her *Young Naturalist's Guide to Flora and Fauna* open to one of the many dog-eared pages. She looks up, giving me one of her warm, soft Anna smiles. But she can't muffle her cough with a handkerchief this time. It makes the whole bed shake.

3

SISTER CONSTANCE HAS MADE a new rule. It happened after Benny found one of the chickens torn apart just after breakfast. He came screaming into the kitchen with the dead bird, making its dead wings flap, shaking its dead head, sending Sister Mary Grace into the pickling room in tears. Sister Mary Grace is the youngest nun, in charge of cooking and cleaning. She's not that much older than Anna, and Anna would cry too, if she saw a dead, bloody bird. Then Sister Constance scolded Benny and told Thomas to bury the bird in the grassy patch of land behind the barn, while she drummed on a tea tin at lunch to get our attention.

"No children are allowed beyond the kitchen terrace, on account of the foxes," she said.

But after lunch, I sneak beyond the terrace anyway.

I want to watch Thomas bury the bird. The others are scared of him, though he is only twenty—barely a man. Benny says he is a monster. But Sister Constance says God gave Thomas only one arm for a reason, and that reason was so that he couldn't go fight the Germans like the other young men in the village, so that he would stay here with us, in the hospital, and take care of the chickens and the sheep and the turnip patch, so that we would have vitamins to keep us strong. I know that Sister Constance can't lie because she's a nun, but, sometimes, I'm scared of Thomas too. Which is why I hide behind the woodpile while I watch him bury the dead chicken.

It's the start of December, and the ground is hard, and it must be difficult for him to dig with one arm, but he manages. Where the other arm should be there is only a sleeve fastened to his shoulder with a big silver diaper pin. He lays the dead chicken in the hole. When he thinks no one is looking, he runs his fingers over the chicken's white, white feathers, and I wonder if it feels the same on his fingers as it would on mine, if soft feathers feel the same for Benny and Anna and Sister Constance and Thomas and me, or if it's only beneath my hands that chickens feel warm and alive, like stones left in the sun. Then Thomas buries the bird under red dirt, and the bird is gone.

4

DR. TURNER COMES EVERY Wednesday to administer
our medication in the little room that was once a butler's
pantry. "Tell me how you are feeling, Emmaline," he says
kindly. Everything about Dr. Turner is kind. The way he
warms his stethoscope before he presses it against my skin.
The chocolate squares he slips me when Sister Constance
isn't looking. The wink he gives me with his woolly gray
caterpillar eyebrows.

Dr. Turner is like Thomas: He isn't whole. Only whole
men can go to war to fight the Germans. But what Dr.
Turner is missing isn't an arm or a leg or even a finger. It's
a part of his heart. It's the daughter and wife he lost to
the bombs. The missing part that makes him twitch when
there is a thunderstorm, and that one time, when lightning

struck the roof and he crawled under the kitchen table and made a strange whining sound like a dog, until Sisters Constance and Mary Grace coaxed him out with weak tea, and sweat was soaking into the armpits of his white coat.

Dr. Turner puts the end of his stethoscope on my back and listens while I breathe. Lining the room, the shelves that used to hold fancy plates are now filled with pill bottles and iodine swabs and tongue depressors.

"Are you taking your medication, Emmaline?"

In the full-length examination mirror behind him, a winged horse is scratching its ear against the window frame.

"Yes, Doctor."

He frowns as if he might not believe me, and then pulls out a pad of paper and a pencil that he wets on his tongue. He turns his back to lean on the cabinet while he writes, and I make a face at the horse; it keeps on scratching its ear. I wonder what it sees, when it looks through the mirror, back at me. I wonder if the mirror-world feels any different from ours: if, over there, cold is still cold, and hot is still hot, and if Sister Constance's rulers really taste as good as the horses make them look.

Dr. Turner finishes writing, folds the note in half, and hands it to me. "Give this to Sister Constance to take to the chemist in Wick."

"Yes, Doctor."

"And paste this outside your door. I noticed the last one fell off."

He hands me a blue ticket. He uses the tickets so the Sisters will know what treatment we need each week. There are three colors: Blue for patients who are well enough to go outside for exercise and fresh air. Yellow for those who must limit their activity to indoors. Red for the ones—the *one*, because it is only Anna—too ill to leave their beds.

Dr. Turner starts to leave, distracted, and I clear my throat loudly so that I'm sure he will hear. He pats his jacket pocket. "Ah. Almost forgot." He hands me a chocolate wrapped in tinfoil, just like the soldiers get in their ration packs. "Our little secret, yes?"

I smile.

I am very good at secrets. I haven't told anyone about the time I saw Jack peeing on a hedgehog by the woodshed, and he let me play with his Lionel steam engine if I stayed quiet.

Well, now you know, but you can keep a secret too. I can tell.

Dr. Turner consults his list. "Send in Kitty next."

I slip off the examination table and pop my head into Sister Constance's classroom, where she is giving the little ones their spelling lesson, to tell Kitty it's her turn. Then I march down the hall. We older children don't have our lessons until the afternoon, so my time is my own, for a little while at least. The mirrors here are empty, but the floors shake, and I wonder if winged horses are walking down it in their world behind the mirrors, or if it is just Thomas banging around on the furnace below. I match the *thunk-thunk-thunk* with my steps until I reach the narrow staircase. I peek over my shoulder for any wild-dog boys with parted red hair. Clear. I dart up the stairs, past the residence level, then up again toward the attic, start unwrapping Dr. Turner's chocolate, and I am just about to take a bite when a face jumps out of the shadows.

I scream.

Benny laughs in his shrill way. Jack comes out from the other side of the rafters, laughing hard, holding in his sides as if scaring me is so funny that his ribs ache because of it.

"You can't be up here!" I say. "You're supposed to be helping in the kitchen until afternoon lessons!"

Benny rests a hand on the stairwell eave and leans over me. "Same goes for you, flea."

I press a hand against my tufts of hair. "I *don't* have fleas."

Benny's favorite Popeye comic book rests on the stairs by his feet. There is a faint smell of smoke. I don't know where Benny and Jack got a cigarette. Not even Dr. Turner can find cigarettes for sale in Wick.

I let my hand fall angrily. "Sister Constance will skin you alive when I tell her you've been smoking up here."

Benny's eyes go dark and his nose gets extra houndlike and I start to shrink an inch or two, but then he glances down and scoops up something lying next to the comic book. "What's this?"

"Another secret?" he sneers. *"You're terrible at keeping secrets."*

A flash of silver wrapper. *My chocolate!*

"Give that back!"

He holds it high, shaking his head as his eyes light up. "Who'd you swipe it from, flea?"

"I didn't steal it! Someone gave it to me, but I can't tell you who!"

"Another secret?" he sneers. "You're terrible at keeping secrets."

"Am not!" I snatch for it. "Give it back!"

But his eyes are on fire. Chocolate means the same thing to him as it does to me—to all of us. A break from dry bread and soupy beans. A sweet memory, something just for you, something from before.

Benny suddenly pinches me just below my shirtsleeve. I yelp, but he only twists harder. He is thin for a boy of thirteen, but strong. "Promise you won't tell Sister Constance about the cigarette."

"Ow!"

"Say it."

"It's mine! Give it back or I'll tell!"

I can feel Jack pacing at the edge of the stairs like a wild dog. He snakes out a hand and pinches my other arm, too, and then snickers.

"Promise you won't tell her, and I'll give you your chocolate back," Benny says.

"Ow! Fine."

He gives me one more sharp pinch and then lets me go.

I pull back, rubbing the red welts on my arm. Jack is grinning with his yellow teeth, so excited that he starts coughing and has to double over.

I hold out my hand.

Benny just smiles slowly.

He tears off the rest of the wrapper and pops it in his mouth. "Waat choholaat?" he mumbles, while lines of brown spit dribble down his chin.

Now I grow an inch, two, three, until my anger towers over him.

"I hate you!" I shove him, but he just laughs, and I run down the stairs. I run past Dr. Turner's old butler's pantry, where little Arthur who never talks is crying silent tears over an injection he's about to receive, and then down into the kitchen. Sister Mary Grace is bent over a copper pot on the stove. She looks up with a tired face that glistens with steam.

"Emmaline, fetch me an onion from the larder. If you dig deep, there's still some good ones, when you peel off the outer layers—"

I shove open the back door and run out onto the kitchen terrace. Children are tossing turnips back and forth and trying to juggle. When their backs are turned, I dart around the corner and run to the garden wall, even though it's against the rules to go so far.

I don't care about the rules.

I'll take my chances with the foxes.

5

IT IS COLD OUTSIDE, and still foggy in the low parts of the fields. I run straight until I reach the gardens' grand front gate, which Thomas padlocked long ago. No one goes beyond the garden wall now. Before the war, the hospital wasn't a hospital at all. It was the house of a beautiful, rich princess, only she was old, and you are probably thinking that doesn't sound like a princess, but it's true. When the bombs started, the princess went to live with relatives and gave the house to the Sisters of Mercy, who added more beds to all of the bedrooms and blacked out the windows with blankets, and the nuns came, and then children came, all on trains. Rumbling, rumbling, while the bombs burst outside. My neighbors were evacuated to Dorset on the first trains. They didn't have the stillwaters. Benny does. Anna does. I do. All the children at Briar Hill hospital have the stillwaters, and so we are here, because we cannot infect each other because we are already infected.

Sister Mary Grace told me that when the princess lived here, the grounds were beautiful. Young men and women from as far as London would come to walk through the walled gardens, amid the rosebushes and statues and gurgling fountains. They used to throw open the ballroom doors so that music would pour onto the sprawling lawns, where her guests would play croquet. But the princess had an army of gardeners, and now we have only Thomas, and Thomas has only his one arm. So that is why the garden gate is locked, and why the little creeping briars grow longer and longer each day.

But the ivy forms a twisting ladder, and it is easy to climb over the garden wall. I just have to tuck my skirt between my legs. On the other side I drop down into a forgotten place. There are benches that are being slowly disappeared by honeysuckle, and crumbling statues of Greek gods with moss clinging to their faces. I wander the maze of walls and find a smaller garden, tucked away in the corner. There is a column in the center that reaches to my shoulders, and on top is a sundial. It has a circular base with a triangular arm pointing toward the sky to cast a shadow that tells the time. It looks to be made of gold or brass that might once have been reflective enough to show the mirror-horses, but now it's too tarnished. I sit on a bench, crunching the vines, and blow into my hands.

Something rustles, and I go stiff.

I haven't forgotten about the foxes.

I hold my breath so it won't cloud in the air and give me away, and listen. *There.* More rustling, just around the corner. Something moving. Can that really be just a fox? And *there.* Back from the direction of the statues. The vines climbing the garden wall tremble suddenly, and I suck in a breath.

That is too big to be a fox.

I go completely still. Except for my breath. Except for my heart. Is this what Papa feels like on the front? That at any moment bullets might splinter the walls? That gas might cloud like morning fog?

Clomp.

I shriek. The ivy trembles violently. Should I run?

Clomp, CLOMP.

It's getting closer! I drop down to the frozen earth. I crawl elbow over elbow through the trenches of dead grass. Benny told us a story once of a German plane that got lost in a storm and crashed on English soil. What if this is a German pilot, lost and angry? My heartbeat thunders in my chest. A willow branch snaps under my elbow, and I shriek.

Clomp, clomp, clomp.

It's a German pilot, I know it, and he's going to have a

gun and he isn't going to listen when I tell him I'm just a girl because he doesn't speak English and he has no way of knowing I'm not a spy!

CLOMP.

He's right around the corner now. There's no time. I grab the snapped willow branch and brandish it, rising to my feet. Foxes or German pilots, Papa would be brave. I must be brave too.

A snort.

A heavy *clomp, clomp, clomp.*

A horse swivels its head around the corner. It is almost entirely white—it has long ropes of silken white mane, and a soft gray muzzle, and wings, snow-white wings, wings that are soft and giant and real.

I drop the willow branch.

"You aren't a German soldier!" I cry.

The horse blinks.

"What *are* you?"

But I know what it is. Oh, I know.

Dry grass itches at my ankles and wind bites at my nose, but all I can do is stare at this horse. It's from the mirror-world. But how did it cross over? And why? The winged horses never leave their world—they barely even glance at me when I tap on the hospital mirrors.

The horse takes a cautious step sideways, its dark eyes fixed on me.

I glance at the golden sundial, but even if it were still

gleaming, the horse is much too large to have squeezed through it. And if it had climbed through any of the mirrors in the hospital, surely we would have heard the crash of broken glass. Perhaps it climbed up through the fountain's reflective water—but no, the horse is not soaked with ice water.

Slowly, I press my hand to my mouth.

What if . . . what if it hasn't crossed over into our world? What if I've crossed over into *its* world?

I pat my dress, my hair, the ivy. No, we are in our world. The sky is gray. The ground is gray. My clothes are gray. The world behind the mirror, I think, would not have so much gray.

The winged horse watches from across the garden, the frozen fountain between us. It snorts loudly, then tears the earth with a hoof the color of quicksilver. Rust-red soil rains against the briars. I think of how when Benny chases me, I run to the kitchen, where the table is an island that keeps him away.

But this horse is not Benny. It has powerful hooves. Powerful teeth. A fountain will not stop it.

I grab the willow branch, brandishing it again.

We stare each other down. My heart *thunk-thunk*s, *thunk-thunk*s, my mind spins. I cannot believe it is here. I cannot believe, even after watching its kind in the mirrors, that it is real.

It lets out another snort, breaking the standoff, and

lurches forward. I clutch the willow branch like a sword, but it doesn't attack. Its neck bends. It noses the fountain. Again. And again.

I lower the branch.

No, it is not a bloodthirsty creature out of one of Benny's stories.

It is only trying to drink.

It looks at me, and I see more clearly this time. It is a girl. It's something in her eyes, a gentleness. I can just tell.

The fountain doesn't flow anymore, but frozen rainwater fills the basin. The horse paws, paws, paws, with her quicksilver hoof. There's a blaze of dark hair between her eyes in the pattern of a star—no, a spark. A tingling feeling spreads through me. All this time, Sister Constance and Dr. Turner were wrong. The winged horses weren't in my imagination. They're real. *She's* real. I want to run back to the hospital on winged feet and tell them all, yell it out, and bring them here. . . .

But no.

No.

I remember Sister Constance's face. Dr. Turner's, too. And the whispers of the other children.

They did not believe me before, and they will not believe me now. That is okay. I am very good at keeping secrets, never mind what Benny says. And this secret—this horse—is my secret. Something just for me.

The horse paws again, muzzle nosing anxiously against

ice. I take a step forward, cautiously, and raise the willow branch. The horse steps back, wary, like a deer at the edge of a wood. I use the branch to bust up the ice in the fountain, *chop, chop, chop* as hard as I can, and then step back quickly to the wall. My heart *thunk-thunk*s. When I look at the horse, my mouth fills with the slightest, barely there taste of ash.

She takes a step forward. And another. Cautious. And then she lowers her head and drinks long and deep from the water beneath the ice. I think she is very thirsty, and that it has been a long time since she has drunk her fill.

6

I LIE AWAKE ALL night wishing there were no such things as schoolwork and supper and silent prayer so I could have stayed with the winged horse.

At first I wonder: How did the horse get into the sundial garden?

And then I remember: She has wings, you dolt, she flew in.

But then I think: Why doesn't she fly away again?

And I start to worry that maybe she has.

So I get up just after dawn and sneak out, even though I know God sees everything and might tell Sister Constance, and I climb over the garden wall with a mealy turnip from the larder in my coat pocket. I'm more and more afraid the winged horse won't be there again, but she is. She is standing by the golden sundial, which is being slowly disappeared by briars, like everything else.

She hears me coming. She stops scratching. She turns her beautiful gray muzzle and looks at me through the mist. She is even more miraculous than I remembered.

"I brought you a treat." My words turn to clouds of mist in the air. I hold out the turnip, but my hand is shaking. I taste ashes in my mouth. The horse is so very beautiful. She's small for a horse, but small things can be lovely, too. Her wings are as white as sugar, and I bet they feel soft and warm, like the chickens.

"Emmaline?"

Someone is calling my name from the hospital. Sister Mary Grace, I think.

The winged horse's eyes go wide and wild. Papa tells stories of horses like this, untamed ones of the plains. He says in America there are whole valleys of horses that have never even seen a person before. The cowboys round them up into giant wooden pens that they keep moving closer and closer, until the horses suddenly find themselves caught. Some are happy to be tamed and pull carts and carry saddles on their backs. But others never are.

"Do you have a name?" I ask.

The winged horse's nostrils flare.

And I notice how she is holding one wing close to her body. I take a step forward, cautiously. The wing's feathers are each the length of my entire arm, the width of my hand. They are packed tightly together, like a shield, and coated with a waxy substance that would make rain roll right off of them. They grow out of the horse's shoulder, and where they meet the bone, the skin is red and swollen.

"What happened to you?"

The horse pauses. Her ears turn back, and then she swivels her beautiful long neck around and swats at a fly on her haunch with her tail. I try to memorize the shape of her back legs—the smooth arcs and long, straight shanks—so that I can draw them later with Anna's colored pencils.

I realize something. "I know why you have come," I tell her. "I think you belong with the other horses, the ones that live in the mirrors, but you've come into our world some-how. Because you're hurt, and you know this is a place of healing. It's okay. No one comes here but me. You can stay as long as you like."

"Emmaline?" Sister Mary Grace calls again. "Are you out here?"

A shadow ripples over the winged horse. A dark one with outstretched wings that swallow up the horse and the sundial. A shrill siren wails to life from the direction of the hospital. The horse's ears go straight, and I turn toward the wailing sound. Its shriek rises and falls.

The air raid siren.

I gape up at the shadow. A plane! The Germans, attack-ing! I drop to all fours and cover my head like they taught us in school. I can't believe the Germans are here, in Shropshire. They bomb cities, not turnip fields. We're supposed to be safe here. The trains, the countryside. It's supposed to be safe.

After a minute no bombs shatter the earth, and I look up. The air raid siren is still wailing and wailing. The winged horse is blinking calmly in the mist.

I was wrong. The dark shadow was far too silent to have been a plane.

And the siren ...

"Drat!" I run toward the garden wall. "Don't worry, it's just a drill," I call over my shoulder to the horse. "*Half an hour, once a week, to keep us sharp and at our peak.*'" As I clamber over the ivy wall, I think of my schoolteacher in Nottingham, waving her hands as we all recited the rhyme together behind our thick rubber gas masks.

The other children are already forming a tidy line on the edge of the kitchen terrace. With their masks on, their faces are black rubber with two gaping eyes and a long round iron snout. Thomas and Sister Constance are helping carry Anna, in the wheeled wicker chair, up the sunken kitchen stairs, though she is attempting to wave them away. She insists she can walk, if they'd only let her. Sister Constance insists she won't allow anyone to fall on stone stairs and crack a head open and ruin her drill.

"Emmaline!" Sister Mary Grace sees me running and presses a hand to her chest in relief, but her face quickly turns to consternation. She holds out my gas mask, which I left dangling on the corner of my bed, and then slides her own over her face.

"I'm sorry, Sister—"

"In line." Her voice has been transformed to that of a creature from outer space. "Go on. Quick feet." She points to the far end of the row of children.

I fumble with the straps and then I am an outer-space creature too. Once we're in line and Anna is up the stairs, Sister Constance stops turning the siren handle. She gives us a sharp nod, and then we march, high knees and pumping fists, around the corner of the house to the sunken entrance of the basement, down the basement stairs, and then sit cross-legged in the straw, staring at each other's masks.

Sister Constance ducks in the doorway with a handheld timer clock. She presses a button.

"Half an hour, children." The straps of her mask make her habit bunch around her face. "No talking. This is time to pray for our soldiers who are fighting on the front."

Then she and Sister Mary Grace are gone, and it is only us twenty small outer-space creatures shifting uncomfortably, coughing behind our masks. Anna, in the wheeled chair, delicately arranges her skirt over her knees. The small girls who are always clinging to each other like three little mice hold hands and play a squeezing game they've never taught anyone else. Peter picks a scab on his elbow.

Children start shifting, trying to keep warm.

Someone coughs loudly.

"Blimey, this is dull," someone else groans, kicking his feet out. Behind the mask, I can't tell if it is Jack or his brother, Peter. "And it was breakfast time, too. The tea will go cold."

"Don't be such a baby, Jack." Benny's thin sneer sounds like he's speaking from the inside of a tin can.

Jack folds his arms. "Or else what?"

Benny sits up straight. "Or else *what*? I'll tell you what." He leans forward, the gas mask making his breathing sound like slow and dangerous waves at sea, out and in, out and in. "Do you know what Captain Cook discovered on his travels in the South Pacific? That cannibals don't like to eat grown-ups. Too tough and chewy. They much prefer children, with their tender flesh. Especially babies who play with toy trains and whine over cold tea. They'd just love *you*."

"That's rubbish," someone says.

Benny spins his rubber face toward the voice, looking from one child to another. "It's true. And if you think you're safe here, you're wrong." His voice drops. "Why do you think Thomas lives out in that little cottage? It's because it's far enough away from the hospital that the Sisters won't hear the screams of the children he snatches."

Anna lets out a snort from behind her mask. "Don't be ridiculous."

Benny ignores her. "He doesn't eat them himself, no."

Everyone's faces are fixed on Benny's. "Though he's tried a bite every now and then, of course—it's hard not to when their meat smells so delicious. He snatches them for the witches that live in the woods. Keeps them in cages in his cottage, feeds them milk to fatten them, just like the lambs, and then delivers them to the witches."

Anna leans forward in her chair tensely. "Stop this at once, or I'll fetch—"

"He took pity on a child once." Benny talks right over her. "A little baby who wailed and wailed, and so he brought it back to its family in Wick. The witches were so cross that they took his arm in its place, as punishment. Cut it off like felling a dead branch."

"That's absurd," Anna says. "He was born without his arm."

But no one is listening to Anna, except for me.

"And that dog. Do you know why he's called Bog? Because he's the one who finds the children, and herds them to the bog to drown them after Thomas fattens them up for the witches."

"Enough!" Anna stands shakily. She pulls off her gas mask. Her curls are wild now, and her face is red from the rubber seals. "Enough, Benny. Not a word of that is true, you're making it up like something out of your comic book, and I'm tired of your stories and—"

A click comes from the basement door. Sister Constance holds the timer clock, its popped button showing that the half hour has passed. Her gas mask is off, and she gives Anna a long look.

Anna quickly sits down in the chair.

"Back upstairs, children," Sister Constance orders.

We file out into the rear lawn with heads hung low, masks dangling from our hands, as we walk back to the kitchen terrace. I toss a look at the garden wall. As soon as I can, I will visit the white horse once more.

And then my eyes settle on Thomas's cottage.

Benny's story isn't true, of course.

It isn't.

Inside, we learn that Jack is right. The tea has gone cold.

7

I SHOULDN'T TELL ANYONE about the horse in the garden.

I shouldn't.

But I've kept the secret all afternoon, and it is gobbling me up like worms on a dead bird. I burst into Anna's room as soon as Sister Constance dismisses class, and find her quietly reading. I jump on the bed and press my lips to her ear.

"There is a white winged horse in the sundial garden," I whisper.

She laughs warmly as my breath tickles her curls, and marks the place in her book with the pink colored pencil and pulls me in close. "My goodness. I thought they were only in the mirrors."

"I thought so too!" I glance at the door. "But one has

There is a white winged horse in the sundial garden.

gotten out. I don't dare tell anyone but you, because they might take her away. And besides, her wing is hurt."

Anna nods slowly, deep in thought. "I suppose she needs you to look after her, then. You took care of your horses back in Nottingham, didn't you? They were bakery horses, you said?" She runs her hand lightly over my hair. "It's rare to see horses in a city these days."

I press my ear against her chest, because I like to hear her heart beating. When I slide lower, her stomach goes *gurgle, gurgle, gurgle,* just like Mama's does.

"Papa looked after them, mostly."

She's stroking my hair softly, looking wistfully out the window. I've never really noticed before that Anna's window looks out onto Thomas's cottage and the turnip patch, so she must spend all day watching him work.

"I'll tell you a secret of my own," she says conspiratorially, "if you promise to keep it to yourself."

I sit up and nod enthusiastically.

"I've never been kissed," she whispers, as her cheeks go as pink as the colored pencil in her book. "Can you believe it? By the time my older sister was sixteen, she was engaged."

She looks back out the window, then her eyes dart, just for a moment, to the red ticket affixed to her open door. I wonder if she is thinking that no one will ever kiss her now, not with the stillwaters. Even the Sisters scrub their hands after touching us.

She gives a sort of a sad laugh that becomes a cough that she muffles in her sleeve. I pat her shoulder gently.

"You'll get better, Anna," I say. "You'll be kissed, I know it. After the war is over, you'll go home and marry a handsome man and have lots of little babies."

Anna takes my hand in hers and gives it a squeeze. Then she looks down at the naturalist book in her lap, and runs her fingers softly down the cover. "And you?" she asks. "What are you going to do when you are better?"

I shrug. "I don't know."

My sister, Marjorie, wants to study the natural world, like Anna, only she'd rather collect stray animals than read about them. In Nottingham she feeds an endless stream of cats. Mama puts up with it only because they kill the mice that gnaw through flour sacks. (Mama doesn't know that Marjorie feeds the mice, too.) Marjorie would probably like to work here at the hospital, tending to us as though we were helpless cats too.

"Perhaps you'll become a baker, like your parents," Anna says. "All those rolls and loaves of bread. You'll puff up like a little pig." She pokes at my ribs teasingly, but I don't smile. The bakery feels so very far away in this moment. I am already forgetting the sounds of Mama humming as she kneads dough.

I shake my head.

"Well, think about what makes you happy," she says.

I think hard.

I like to draw. And to go to the cinema with Marjorie—
Heidi is the best movie I've seen. I like to climb the garden
wall even though Sister Constance told us not to. And I like
the winged horse. Yes, that is what makes me happy. That
she is mine. That she is secret.

"I'd like to be an explorer," I say at last. "I'd like to
discover new things that no one else has. Go places other
people won't."

And then I feel embarrassed, because it is a silly wish.
Explorers are brave, dashing men who fly airplanes and hunt
Germans and have lungs that aren't choked with stillwaters.

Anna blinks in surprise, and then the most beautiful
smile crosses her face. "But, Emmaline," she says, "you already *are.*"

8

"EMMALINE'S BEEN OUTSIDE! Look at her dress!"

Benny jumps up from the breakfast table the next morning and points to the back of my skirt. I reach around and feel a briar. *Drat.* There are only briar bushes in one place—the gardens—and it must have caught yesterday during my visit to the white horse. Sister Constance rubs her tired eyes and gives me her *God would disapprove* look.

"Emmaline, remember the rule. It's for your own good, with the foxes out there, growing hungrier as it gets colder." She shakes her head, muttering something about how fresh air won't cure any of us if we freeze to death first.

I sit at the table and eat my porridge with plum jam. Most of the younger children's seats are empty, their bowls already licked clean. Only Benny, and Jack and his brother

Peter, and the three small girls who are always clinging to each other remain. Thomas is at the far end of the long table, where the adults eat, hunched over his bowl like a piece of twisted driftwood that has somehow washed up in our breakfast room. His arm-side is facing me, and if I lean forward a little, I can almost pretend his other arm is there, just hidden.

I eye him sideways. He doesn't look like the type to fatten children for witches, but who does?

"Where'd you go, then, Emmaline?" Benny asks, his head jutted forward. "To the loo outside? I bet you like to feel fresh air on your bum."

Jack snickers. The three little mice do too.

"That's a lie!" I say. My head whips toward the kitchen pantry door, but Sister Constance is cataloging cans inside and hasn't heard this injustice. "I was in the sundial garden. I found a winged horse there—"

I clamp a hand over my mouth.

So much for keeping secrets.

Benny starts laughing. "A *what*? A flying horse?" He pretends to laugh so hard that he has to grip the edge of the table to keep from falling off the bench. But then the still-waters rise up and he coughs and coughs, and it sounds like a dog barking in the night.

Jack jumps in. "Winged horses don't exist, flea."

"They did!" one of the mice pipes up. "In the Bible they lived in the Garden of Eden, but then the great flood came and there wasn't any room left on Noah's ark, so they drowned. That's why there aren't any more of them."

Even doubled over in pain, Benny manages to shoot the little mouse a sneer. "That's unicorns." He coughs more. "And it isn't true, anyway. It's just something Sister Mary Grace made up to make you pay attention in church."

The little mouse sulks back to her porridge.

"They *do* exist," I say. "Only not in our world. They live in the other world, the one behind the mirrors. You would see them, if you ever looked, but I can tell from your greasy hair that you haven't laid eyes on a mirror in days. Anyway, the horse in the sundial garden got out somehow."

The other children are quiet. The only sound is Thomas's metal spoon, scraping the last of his porridge at the far end of the table.

"I'll prove it," I say. "Come and see."

"And how are we supposed to do that?" Benny tries to twist the words into a sneer, but the truth is, I think he's a little curious. "We aren't allowed that far, and anyway, the garden gate is locked."

"You're a boy. If I can climb over the wall in a dress, you can." I give him a hard look. "Are you afraid of the foxes?"

Benny glances in the direction of the pantry. "Of course not."

The three little mice confer among themselves in their secret mouse language. Thomas stands up and dumps his bowl in the soapy dishwater, and they hush. I think they forgot he was there, so silent and flat, as unnoticeable as the shadows that have been cast on the wall this whole time. He wipes his one hand on a kitchen towel, and then hitches up his trousers with all the grace of a bear.

"We'd better not," announces Kitty, the leader of the mice. Her eyes are on Thomas as the wooden kitchen door smacks shut behind him. "Besides, they really *don't* exist, Emmaline. It's just a game you're playing."

Benny reclines, folding his arms as though, now that Thomas is gone and the Sisters aren't present, he is the ruler of the breakfast table. "There's a war on, Emmaline. It might have been fun to make things up before, but we have to grow up now. In war there are no children. Only adults." Seeming very satisfied with himself, he licks the jam off of his thumb.

I push to my feet. Don't they even want to see? The winged horse is right there, just on the other side of the garden wall. I set my bowl angrily by the kitchen sink, and then storm out onto the terrace.

It is cold, and I didn't bring my coat, but I don't want to go back inside with Benny and his talk about growing up and war. I sit on the highest of the kitchen steps, hugging my arms tight, worried for the winged horse. But it is starting to rain, and I can't escape now.

"Emmaline."

I straighten toward the voice. It's Thomas, his one arm holding a shovel, ropes slung around the shoulder with the pinned-up sleeve. I overheard the Sisters talking about Thomas in the larder one time, while I was taking a nap on the flour sacks. *It can't be easy for him,* Sister Constance said. *His father's made such a name for himself, in the last war and now in this one, too. And here Thomas is, shoveling turnips all day, no girls to be sweet on except poor dying Anna and a couple of nuns.*

"Emmaline," Thomas says again.

"What?"

"I see the winged horses too."

My heart goes *thump, thump, thump.* I'm not the only one! But I look away, because Thomas is like the shadows on the wall. Dark and ever-present, and just a little bit scary. I know Benny's stories about him aren't any more true than the story in the pages of his comic book. I know this. And yet, if anyone else is going to be a part of my secret world, I do not think I want it to be Thomas.

9

IT RAINS FOR DAYS and days. It is a sleeting kind of rain that wants to be snow but can't figure out how to turn white and fluffy, and so it just slaps against the windows. There is no escaping to see the white winged horse. I can only hope she is all right.

I lie on my bed at night, drawing with chalk by the light of a fat candle because Anna only lets me use her colored pencils when I am in her room. It's cozy here, beneath the attic eaves. I was the last to arrive at Briar Hill. All the beds were taken, and Thomas had to clear out one of the attic rooms and make this bed out of wood and rope. Little bits of straw poke through the mattress and itch my skin. I like the smell, though. It reminds me of home. Of Nutmeg and Ginger, and of Spice, throwing their heads to shake out their dark manes as soon as Papa takes off their harnesses, in just the same way Papa tosses his own hair when he takes off his baker's cap.

I've drawn the horse's ears right at last, I think, but her wing is giving me trouble—it hangs limply in my drawing just as it does in the real world. Outside, lightning crashes, and my hand jerks and draws a snaking white line. The thunder takes its time rolling in. You can tell how far away a storm is by how many seconds pass between lightning and thunder. *Three, four,* I count, and then it comes. Four. Four miles off.

I shove the chalk in my pocket and push open the curtain.

All I can see of the garden is charcoal-colored shadows slick with moisture, and the blowing skeletons of trees. I cannot see the winged horse, but I can feel her. Does the storm frighten her?

Lightning strikes again.

One. Two.

Then thunder.

Two miles off now. I shove back the curtain and sprawl on the bed. The candle flame flickers, then straightens as the wind howls.

I reach for my chalk, and suddenly thunder crashes even louder.

I shriek and huddle under my quilt. There was no counting. No miles. The storm is right on top of us! The wind howls louder still as it rips open the window. A freezing gust comes barreling in, rain and ice and everything in between. The candle flickers wildly and goes out. I tumble toward the window, knocking the candle to the floor. The storm isn't allowed in my bedroom; neither is the night.

Icy rain streaks my hair and face. Lightning flashes again, and for a moment, the night world is mine to see. Quaking branches throwing themselves on the wind's mercy. Bare fields stretch into night.

Acorns drop onto the roof like a volley of bullets. *Rat-a-tat. Rat-a-tat.* And then it's dark again. Really dark. Black.

I shove the window closed and twist the lock. When I blink, crystals clink together. The attic is nothing but shadows and the smell of extinguished fire. I feel for the quilt.

RAT-A-TAT.

More sounds, louder. It's too late in the year to be acorns. Something is stomping, clomping, thumping, on the sloping roof.

I know that sound.

Horses.

Outside, the wind howls louder. Only a horse with wings could get up three stories to stomp on the roof. Is it the one from the garden, prancing? But no, this is gnashing. This is pawing. This is the *rat-a-tat* of guns, only it is a horse tearing at the roof.

I take a step backward.

This can't be *my* winged horse.

My winged horse is chicken feathers and a soft gray muzzle. My winged horse is a blaze the shape of a spark.

Clomp. Clomp. Clomp.

Thunder comes again, and something cracks in the roof, as though whatever is on the other side is trying to tear its way in. I back up against the bed and trip over the fallen candle.

Forget it!

I grab my coat, throw open the door, and gallop down the stairs and straight into Anna's room. She jerks upright at the sound, sweaty hair plastered to the side of her face, eyes squinting. I jump on the bed next to her and burrow under the covers.

"Emmaline! What's the matter? Why are you wet?" She pushes the hair out of her face. "Have you been outside, you mad child?"

Her bed is warm. Her bed is safe. The attic is far away, and the roof with the shaking rafters and the stomping horse is even farther. I take a long, deep breath. Icy rain and wind push at her bedroom window, but muffled by the wool blanket, it seems like only a storm. "The wind blew my window open."

"I've a towel on the—"

"There was something out there, Anna. On the roof. I think another one of the winged horses has crossed over from the mirror-world. A bad one."

In the darkness, I cannot see her face. She switches on her light, and then studies me with frowning eyes. She glances at the small oval hand mirror on her bedside table. It reflects a small sliver of the window that the wool blanket hasn't quite covered; a slice of the outside, which is dark now.

"I thought it was the one from the garden," I continue, "but it can't be because her wing is hurt and she can't fly. It was so loud, pawing and pawing like it was angry. Didn't you hear it?" She is still looking at the mirror, oddly, as though her thoughts are elsewhere. "Anna, didn't you hear it?" I shake her by the sleeve.

She blinks. "No. But . . . I'm all the way down here on the second floor, and your room is right beneath the roof. Are you certain it wasn't branches falling?"

"I need to check on the horse in the garden. Something awful might have happened to her." When I start to roll out of bed, Anna snaps upright and grabs me.

"You can't! You'll freeze out there."

"She's all alone!"

She holds me firmly. "Well, you can check on her in the morning. You won't be able to help her if you catch fever. Now fetch that towel from the banister, and put on these socks. You're shaking."

She dries my hair with the towel, and wipes the ice off my eyelashes. I keep looking at that sliver of night reflected in the mirror. Waiting to see a flash of wings and kicking hooves. But there is nothing.

Nothing.

Nothing.

Anna switches off the lamp and turns her back to me, but then after a few moments rolls over and interlaces her fingers with my own. She gives my hand a squeeze. Once she falls asleep, I can feel her temperature rise, night sweat soaking into the sheets. I drift off to the sound of twenty children coughing in their sleep, and I think about the white winged mare, of lightning, and of *rat-a-tat* hooves.

10

SOMETIME IN THE NIGHT, the rain turns to snow. At first light, Anna and I push our faces against the bedroom window, watching it come down in quiet flakes. It is thicker here than I ever saw in Nottingham, where city snow quickly turns slushy and brown. The whole world outside is still, except for Thomas trudging through the snow to bring the sheep into the barn, and Bog, who nips at the sheep's backsides.

"Can I borrow your mittens?" I ask Anna.

"You're still going there, even though you know you shouldn't?"

"I have to."

She squints into the bright world outside. Thomas and Bog are rescuing one of the lambs, which has managed to wedge itself between two fence posts. Thomas's cheeks are red, and his breath puffs in the air, but then he manages to free the sheep, scooping it up with just his one arm, and tossing it over the fence, where it goes stumbling through the snow to its mama sheep.

"Then I'm coming too," Anna says.

"You mustn't! You're sick."

"So are you, you naughty goose. I'm tired of this bed, and I'm not a complete invalid, no matter what Dr. Turner says. I want to walk in the snow." Slowly, frailly, she makes her way over to the cedar chest at the foot of the bed. Just that effort puts her out of breath, though she tries to hide it. Out come woolen mittens and hats and scarves that are all a dull shade of gray. She starts to wind a scarf around my neck.

"The stitches are all uneven," I mumble as I shrug on my coat and do up the buttons.

"The Americans sent them for the war effort. Poor dears, Americans can't knit to save their lives, though I suppose it's good of them to try. Now, put these mittens on and show me how you're always sneaking around without the Sisters noticing." She pulls a hat over her own curls, glancing in the mirror to adjust them, then takes her coat off the hook behind her door.

The only other person awake this early, judging by the sound, is Sister Mary Grace, getting breakfast ready in the kitchen. So we tiptoe like stealthy cats down the stairs and along the hallway to the library. There is a door the Sisters keep locked, but the lock on the middle window is broken. I push the window open. We climb out into the scrubby boxwood bushes. We have to leave the window ajar to get back in, but the wool blanket hides the evidence.

The cold air hits us. Anna's cheeks are already splotchy with red. I worry that this isn't wise, her leaving her warm bed and the cups of tea brought to her. Her arms and legs are so painfully thin. The covers usually hide them, but now, against the bricks of the hospital, she seems so fragile, a girl made of twigs.

"Go on, then," she says. "I want to meet this magic horse of yours." She cranes her neck in the direction of the barn, and her voice rises a little. "Do you think we'll run into Thomas?"

"Not if we can help it."

She looks disappointed.

I start sneaking along the row of boxwoods and, once I'm certain the coast is clear, dart across the rear lawn to the garden wall. Anna shuffles behind me. She's quick and light as a curled leaf, but her breathing is shallow and fast. She leans against the ivy, a mittened hand pressed to her chest. I can hear the rumble starting there. She leans over and coughs into the snow so hard I'm afraid she'll tear something.

"Anna—"

"I'm fine."

"I think you should—"

"I'm fine!" She turns abruptly. "What in heavens is *that*?"

I tip my head up to see what she is looking at. The roof. A foot of snow sits on top like the icing Mama slathers on frosted cakes, only there is a patch where the snow has been disturbed violently. And there are prints. The shape is unmistakable.

"See!" I cry. "Hoofprints!"

Anna doesn't stop staring at the roof. Her eyes narrow like she's on the verge of remembering something, but then a gritty sound climbs up her throat, and she doubles over in coughs. They shake her hard, which shakes the ivy, and a dusting of snow powders the air. Her hat goes tumbling off.

Suddenly Bog comes thundering around the corner of the gardens, barking like mad. We've been discovered. In another second Thomas trudges round. He stops when he sees us. Bog keeps barking until Thomas gives a sharp *sss*, and he sits right on cue.

Anna reaches for the ivy, trying to pull herself back up. "Look!" she says in a weak voice. "On the roof."

Thomas doesn't glance at the roof as he comes forward to help her stand up. "Yes, I saw those marks this morning, but really, you shouldn't be out here, Miss Anna. You'll catch cold. Emmaline, get her hat."

"Emmaline is going to . . . show me the sundial garden."

"Not today she isn't, not with you looking like that."

I stand on tiptoe to put Anna's hat back on her head. I try to angle it the way she likes, so the curls show.

"Maybe another day, Emmaline," Anna says. "I so badly want to see that horse of yours."

But the spirit is out of her. Her face is a paler shade than I have ever seen it. Her arms are a thin layer of skin over brittle bone. I think there is more stillwater in her veins now than blood.

Thomas looks back at me. "Are you coming, Emma-line?"

I shake my head.

"Promise you won't stay out long, then," he says. When I nod, Thomas helps her back toward the house.

Bog and I watch their two brown coats against the snow. They move slowly, as though each step is an effort. I do not think Anna will talk about walking in snow again.

Thomas whistles, and Bog leaves me too.

11

I CLIMB OVER THE garden wall and drop to the other side. I am a little scared of what I will find. *Could* it have been my winged horse up on the roof, gnashing with hooves, her wing not as wounded as I'd thought? What if she has never seen snow before and thinks little pieces of the sky are falling, that the clouds are getting shorn like sheep?

The snow forms deep drifts in the gardens that swallow my ankles. All the grays and browns of our world are gone now, replaced by white. Maybe this is what the winged horse's world is like all the time. Beautiful and white, soft and cold. Maybe she feels more at home now, in the storm, than she ever has before. I shake the cold from my hands as I peek around the corner into the sundial garden.

She is there.

I feel my chest lift with relief and the wonder of her.

She is standing in the lee of the highest wall, the only protection from the snow, though it isn't much. Her wings are tucked into her sides but pulsing slightly, as if she wants to take off but can't. Puffs of steam blow from her nostrils. Her feet are nimble and anxious, as though she's never walked in snow.

No, this is not familiar to her. Whatever snow is like in her world, it isn't this stretch of colorless blank.

I step on an old turnip and yelp, and her head swivels toward me.

Her eyes are so wide that I can see the whites of them. She skitters back into the corner, and she paws harder, boxed in. I hold my hands out so she knows I am no threat.

"Easy. Easy."

Sometimes our horses back in Nottingham would get spooked. They were used to storms, but not bombs. Their eyes would roll, and they would kick the doors of their stalls, wanting to be set free. But Papa was away at war, and we couldn't let them out or they would run wild through the streets and never come home. Marjorie would climb into bed with me and hold me tight, singing in my ear so we wouldn't hear their cries.

I try to take a step forward, but the winged horse snorts in protest. She has pawed the snow in her corner of the garden into a muddy mess. But her prints are small and dainty, not at all like the rough marks on the roof.

But if it wasn't her ...

The willow stick still rests on the fountain. I take a careful step to the left, moving very slowly so I do not scare her, and break up the frozen water again so that she can drink, and then set the stick back down. Mud has dulled her color. Beneath it, I know she is as white as chicken feathers, and just as soft. I ache to brush away the dirt and press my cheek to her side, feel the rise and fall of her breath, tend to her hurt wing like Mama does whenever I have a bruise. Her eyes are still wide, but they have stopped rolling. She lifts her right foot, and then sets it down.

Papa says you cannot rush a horse to be broken, or else it will be just that—broken.

We stand looking at one another, each of us taking in the other. I do not come closer, and she does not panic. We are just two warm bodies in the snow. I have heard that horses can smell whether a person is gentle or not. I imagine it is a scent like flowers, maybe lavender or Russian sage, but not roses, because even horses know that roses have thorns.

A gust of wind blows, and something flutters beneath the sundial. Paper. Someone has tucked a note beneath the sundial's golden arm. Who else has been here? Did Benny finally get up the courage? Or the three little mice?

I tiptoe through the snow at the speed of growing ivy, until I can pull out the paper.

It is soggy with snow. It's been here all morning, I think. The paper is thick, like the kind Dr. Turner uses for his prescriptions, but there is a silken red ribbon tied around it. I glance at the horse. She is watching me, breathing steam, as I untie it with numb fingers.

To whoever receives this message,

    I am in desperate need of assistance. I have brought this horse to your world because her wing is broken, and I need a safe place to hide her. You see, she is being pursued by a dark and sinister force from our world—a Black Horse who hunts by smell and moonlight—and she cannot fly away to escape him. My own crossings between worlds are limited, and I would be forever in your debt if you would watch over her until I can return.

                           Ride true,
                           The Horse Lord

Postscript: Her name is Foxfire. She likes apples.

A letter from the world behind the mirrors! The Horse Lord himself—I didn't even know there *was* a Horse Lord! Wind pushes at the letter. It is so cold that my eyes water and make the script swim, but I blink away the cold and read it again. No wonder she hasn't touched my turnips— she likes apples. The handwriting is careful and lovely, with little flourishes at the ends of the *t*'s just like Anna makes. In my excitement, I crumple the letter accidentally, and then smooth it out the best I can.

"Foxfire?" I say to the winged horse. "That's your name?"

She doesn't answer; but then again, she is a horse. She turns toward the fountain. I step back. She comes forward cautiously, dipping her head to drink. Her muscles ripple beneath snow-white horseflesh. There are no markings on her girth or back from where a saddle would rub. She is wild, and too proud to have a master, so I think the Horse Lord must be more like a guardian. I imagine him to be a young and handsome prince, who takes care of the wild winged horses of his world.

She is closer now, as she drinks. I can see the muscles of her neck moving. If I took a few steps forward and reached out a hand, I could touch her. But I don't. She wouldn't let me, not yet. I have to earn her trust.

A dark shadow passes overhead. The same silent shadow as before, with outstretched wings, that I mistook for a German plane. Foxfire looks up through the snow. Her ears turn back. Somehow, we are linked—I feel her fear within me.

Overhead the shadow is circling, circling.

Only now I recognize the outline. The horses I've seen in the mirrors have been all different colors: white and dappled and chocolate brown, but never black. Until now.

Flying through the storm like thunder embodied, circling like a crow, searching for Foxfire.

This is the dark presence the Horse Lord warned against. The gnashing beast on the roof.

The Black Horse.

I flip over the Horse Lord's letter and take out my chalk, still in my pocket from last night. It makes fat lines, but I don't need to say much.

I accept.—*Emmaline May*

12

I STAND OUTSIDE of the barn with my arms hugged tightly around my chest. Inside, someone is pounding a hammer. *Thwack. Thwack. Thwack.* I take a deep breath and push open the door.

Thomas sees me and stops repairing the broken kitchen bench, which he has already repaired three times before. He's sweating with the effort and his dark hair is smeared across his face and I suddenly don't want to be here, but I promised the Horse Lord.

"Did you need something, Emmaline?"

His voice isn't as angry as the tight set of his face. I point to the bucket of old apples Thomas gives the sheep. "May I have one of those?"

His eyebrows knit together, but then he sets down the

hammer and digs around in the bucket until he finds a good one. He starts to hand it to me, but at the last minute gives me a suspicious look. "This wouldn't be for the winged horse in the sundial garden, would it?"

I eye him warily. He said that he'd seen the winged horses too, but Thomas is practically an adult. If Benny and the three little mice won't even believe me, why would he? But Thomas's face is very serious. It's a plain kind of face. His chin is rather weak, and his forehead stretches for miles when he brushes his sweaty hair back like that. But he has nice eyes. They are green, like mine.

I take the apple. "Have you really seen the winged horses?"

He picks his hammer up again. "Yes."

"In the mirrors?"

"In the frozen lake on the Mason farm, just beyond the back fields. When the sun shines, the ice is like a mirror, and you can see them plain as day."

I run my finger along the dusty edge of his workbench. "I know what caused the hoofprints on the roof after the snowstorm," I tell him. "There's another horse that's crossed through the mirror. A black one. I got a special letter about it. Have you seen him?"

Thomas wipes the sweat from his forehead again. "Not yet, no."

"Well, be careful. He is a dark and sinister force."

Thomas raises an eyebrow. Then he nods toward Bog, who is asleep, dreaming dog dreams, by a stack of pine boxes. "I wouldn't worry too much about the Black Horse. If he gets close, Bog will bark like mad. He scares away the foxes. He can scare away anything."

I like Bog. He's a smart dog, and he'll chase after a stick if you throw it, but I don't think all the barking in the world could scare away the Black Horse.

"Thank you," I say. "For the apple."

"Give my regards to the winged horse in the sundial garden. I haven't seen him, but I think I've heard him moving around. Tell him I hope his wing heals soon."

"It's a girl," I say. "Her name is Foxfire."

He pauses the hammer. "My mistake." And then, "A good name, for a good horse."

I stand up, hugging my arms against the cold, and then I think of something. "How did you know about her broken wing?"

Thomas swings the hammer with his one arm. "Well." He swings the hammer again. *Thwack.* "If she didn't have a broken wing, she would have flown away."

I reach into my pocket and rub the Horse Lord's ribbon between my fingers.

Maybe Thomas sees the winged horses because he didn't go off to war like the other young men in the village. Maybe missing the war means he hasn't entirely grown up. And yet, as he swings that hammer, there is something about him that is like the twisting old oaks on the front lawn—ancient and knowing.

13

DR. TURNER CANNOT COME to the hospital on account of the snow. Sister Constance rings up the chemist in Wick who delivers our medications once a week, but he can't make it either, so Sister Constance has to borrow the donkey that lives on the Mason farm, and the cart, and ride into Wick on her own. It's funny to see her in her black nun's habit, under a thick coat and four layers of blankets, steering a rickety old donkey through the snow. I laugh, but Anna chides me.

"Hush, Em. Would *you* rather make the trip to Wick?"

I sigh. Then Anna starts coughing into her handkerchief and I feel awful, because out of all of us, Anna is the one who needs the medicine most.

She suddenly lurches forward in bed, coughing harder

than ever. I pick up the colored pencils and my latest drawings, because they're really the best drawings of Foxfire I've done, and I'd hate for them to get ruined. Anna's whole body is shaking now each time she coughs, and her face has gone very white. Not white like snow, or Foxfire's wings, but a translucent, greasy kind of white like the rancid lard Sister Mary Grace throws out.

Anna removes her handkerchief away from her mouth, and we stare at it, then at each other.

There's a spot of red.

Blood.

"Fetch Sister Mary Grace," she says.

Her voice wavers and there are tears in her eyes. I scramble off the bed with pages and pages of drawings in my arms, and think I should leave them, no, I should just go, and end up dropping everything in the hallway outside and tripping over it all as I run downstairs to the kitchen. Sister Mary Grace is just making our afternoon tea, and the kettle is starting to steam.

"It's Anna!" I say. "I think she's dying!"

Sister Mary Grace drops the butter knife and grabs a kitchen towel, then runs past me up the steps toward Anna's room. The kettle is whistling now. I hear murmurs of the other children—they've probably heard the commotion and are popping their heads out of their rooms like birds peeking out of their nests, curious. The kettle is whistling louder. I should go back to Anna's room, but I don't want to. I don't want to see the blood. I don't want to hear that coughing, that coughing, mixed with her tears. In the hallway, my drawings are scattered like autumn leaves, half crumpled underfoot. Ruined, but I don't care anymore.

Benny comes charging into the kitchen and jerks the screaming kettle off of the stove. I can smell metal burning. I expect him to yell at me for letting it boil clean dry of water, but he doesn't. He sets it on a wooden trivet and gives me one long look, and then his eyes flick to the stairs, where we can both hear Anna's bone-deep coughs.

"You should have left it," I say. "You should have let it keep whistling."

"Emmaline—" His voice, for once, isn't a sneer.

He's seen my tears. But I don't want his pity! I shove past him and run outside into the frozen world of snow and ice. Cold stings my bare hands—I've forgotten my coat, but I can't go back. I run and run though my lungs scream at me to stop. When the princess had this place built, did she imagine that one day children would die here, crying so loud you could hear it even over a screaming kettle? Did she think, while she threw open the doors and let music pour onto the back lawn, that one day a black winged horse would circle around and around the roof, tirelessly, always on the hunt?

I collapse in the snow. The coughing fit hits me hard.

The barn door is ajar. Steam is coming from the crack. I pull it open to investigate, cautiously, in case Thomas is there, but it is only the sheep. They are pressed so tightly together, and there are so many of them, that their heat makes the barn as warm as toast from the oven. I crawl over the stall gate and curl up in the middle of them, in the straw and wool and breathing bodies, and at last feel warm.

14

WHEN I WAKE, I am in my own bed.

My sheets are soaked with sweat. I don't know who found me in the barn and brought me back. My dreams were coffee-scented, and Thomas is the only one who drinks coffee, though Benny takes a sip every now and then and pretends he likes it. But I can't picture a one-armed man carrying me, even though I saw him pick up that lamb and throw it over the fence into its pasture. I wrap a blanket around my dress and shuffle down the stairs and hover outside of Anna's room. The door is open a crack. Sister Mary Grace is there, tidying up spilled broth.

I can see the bedsheets rising and falling as Anna breathes. She is asleep. *Alive.* Voices come from downstairs. Sister Constance must be back with the medicine.

I've slept through supper, but the Sisters have left me some ham beneath a napkin. As I sit alone at the kitchen table and eat, something moves in the reflection of the copper teakettle. The angles of the kitchen are warped in its curving sides, so that the ceiling looks tiny, and the fireplace inflates into a roaring inferno behind me. My nose is the size of a swollen plum, my eyes unnaturally small. A gray winged horse is nosing around the table behind me, probably hungry for toast with jam. It snuffles against my mirror-chair, then against my mirror-shoulders. I shiver, even though my real shoulders have felt nothing. A stick cracks in the fire, and the horse turns toward it. Afraid of the flames or curious, I am not sure. It stretches its wings so suddenly that I duck.

"Be careful," I whisper. "The fire could burn you."

Does my voice carry to the world beyond the mirror? The gray horse swivels its head to the left, then to the right, then folds its wings and walks into the ground-floor hall.

I push away the kettle. I do not want to see my reflection. The hair that has grown back unevenly. My hand drifts up to untangle the tufts, and I taste ashes that don't have anything to do with the kitchen fire. Even without the kettle's distortions, Benny is right. I do look odd.

Can I tell you a secret?

This is not the first hospital I have been in. I have not always had the stillwaters. That came later, after the fire, after the bandages. After the horses kicking at their stall doors, and no one to let them out.

The kitchen door slams, and the three little mice come in with red cheeks. They've recruited a fourth into their ranks now: Arthur, the blond boy who never speaks and sucks his thumb. They've dressed him as a pirate prince and given him a shiny kitchen ladle as a sword, but he's only gazing at his own reflection in it. Kitty, the leader of the mice, holds up two long black feathers. They look like crow feathers, except they have a sheen like wax and are the length of her arm.

"Look what we found on the terrace!"

She holds one feather in each hand, flapping her arms like a giant bird and cawing at the ceiling, and the girls giggle and run down the hall.

15

WHEN I WAS FIVE, my sister Marjorie found a wounded bird in the street. Our neighbor's cat had gotten it and thrashed it about, before Marjorie chased it off. The bird didn't move, though its heart *flit-flit-flit*ted beneath our fingertips. Its body was so soft, as though just touching it might break something. Marjorie made a cage out of an old sieve and filled it with leaves. We dug through Mama's garden for worms, and chopped them up, and fed them to the bird on the end of a small twig. Our neighbor said the bird would never survive, but Marjorie was patient. Every day, she dug for more worms. After three weeks, the little bird was flapping its wings around, trying to take off in the makeshift cage. We carried the cage to the edge of the empty building behind the bakery. Marjorie opened the door, and the bird flew away.

But Foxfire isn't that little bird. I do not think worms and a bed of leaves will fix her.

She is waiting for me as I crawl over the garden wall. My spine tingles as I meet her eyes. I still can't believe she's real, but here she is, standing in front of me. The torn skin on her right wing is raw, and the dent in the bone looks painful. She tries to stretch out her wings. Her left one will extend, but the right one catches.

"I have something for you," I say softly.

Her ears perk up when my hand goes into my pocket, but her eyes are still wary. She is used to the wind and the sun, not to little girls.

"The Horse Lord wrote me that you liked these." I take out the shiny red apple I got from Thomas. Her ears swivel forward, curious. She raises her right hoof, but then lowers it again. I take a slow step forward, with the apple resting in my flat palm. "It's all right. I'm not going to hurt you. I just want to give you this apple."

When I reach the fountain, my bulky coat knocks off the willow stick, and she jerks at the whip of movement. Her eyes flash their whites.

"Easy, Foxfire."

But the next step I take is too far. She snorts and paws the snow with muddy hooves. Her thick mane flies as she tosses her head, warning me back.

I stop.

Slowly, I crouch to the earth and roll the apple to

her corner of the garden. She stops thrashing. Her eyes never leave me, but she lowers her head. Sniffing. Snorting. Her inquisitive lips grope until they feel the shape of the apple.

She jerks her head up, and munches on it contentedly.

I back up slowly, until I reach the sundial, where there is a new letter tucked under the golden arm, tied in ribbon. I unroll it while Foxfire finishes the apple.

Dear Emmaline May,

I must once again ask you for assistance. Though I thought it impossible, the Black Horse has crossed over into your world and is, at this very moment, in pursuit of Foxfire.

The Black Horse is strong and relentless, but he has one weakness, and it is this: color. Color burns his eyes. The only light he can see by is colorless moonlight—the brighter the moon, the clearer he sees. Tonight, there is a new moon, which means the sky will be dark and he will have to hunt by smell alone. But as the moon grows brighter each night, you must surround Foxfire with colorful objects large enough to be seen from a distance— one for each color of the rainbow—to create a spectral shield that will hide her from his vision even during the brightest full moon.

I beg you to accept this mission of utmost importance.

Ride true,
The Horse Lord

I stare at the letter with wide eyes.

I am to protect Foxfire?

I am to undergo a mission of utmost importance, all on my own? No, no, I can't possibly. Feeding her and caring for her is one thing, but this is quite another. My heart starts to swell with that *rat-a-tat* fear, and I want to crawl over the wall and run, run away from the letter.

But the Horse Lord is depending on *me.*

I hold the ribbon up to the light. If I'm to find colorful objects, then could this be the first? It is thick and long, surely long enough to be seen from a distance. It is red, but looking closer, it is more than that. Sometimes when it catches the light it is cherry red, other times the same red as the emblems painted on the army trucks that rumble by.

Foxfire is still munching on the apple, but her eyes are fastened to the ribbon. I glance at the ivy covering the garden wall. The vines twist around themselves to form little nooks and pockets, like a fairy shelf. I find a sturdy vine and tie the red ribbon around it so that it flickers in the wind. It is bright and shiny against the dull dark green. I take a step back, and then another, and it still shines brightly.

Yes, I think. Yes, maybe I can do this.

But a cloud covers the sun, and I squint up at the sky.

One red ribbon will not be enough.

I must find something blue, and green, and yellow, and all the other rainbow colors in shades bright enough to blind the Black Horse when he comes for Foxfire. And he will come. I know this. Even now I can feel him circling just beyond the clouds. His black hooves tear up wisps of white-gray as he circles and circles, pulling the winds with him, stirring thunder in his wake.

But where to find blues and greens and yellows? The only colors at the hospital are on little paper tickets attached to our doors that would dissolve in the rain. There are no flowers now. No rainbows arching in the sky after an April rain shower.

The last time I saw a rainbow, I was running home with Marjorie after school, darting from doorway to doorway to escape the spring rain. She made it into a game. Water was poison gas; each drip was one day off your life, so we had to run and run and run, before we had no days left. The rain came harder, and she pulled me into the doorway of a theater. "If we don't hide," she said, "We'll have no days left." She hugged me close and pointed above the church, where a double rainbow spanned the steeple. "Look!"

Everything at Briar Hill is white snow and gray stone. It is the dull browns and greens of soldiers' uniforms, and the black of nuns' habits. No wonder we have drawn the Black Horse straight to us. Our world is colorless midwinter.

I close my eyes and think of that day in the rain. Marjorie's bright yellow raincoat. My blue socks. The lively pink in our cheeks, not the burn of fever in Anna's. I take off my mittens and press my cold hands to my face. I miss Marjorie so much, I could cry. I don't know what to do without her singing me to sleep, making games of rainstorms, sneaking me slices of apple pie. It has been so long since I've seen so many colors all together that I'm afraid I might have forgotten them. The only blue I can picture now is a watery sky. The only yellow the murky medicine Dr. Turner gives us. But there must be more out there. There must be brighter things.

Something nudges me from behind.

I turn and gasp. Foxfire is right behind me. Her muzzle is poised to nudge my shoulder again, her warm horse-breath on my neck, her ears swiveled forward. I dare not move, afraid to spook her. She dips her head, horse-lips searching the folds of my coat, until she reaches my pocket. When she discovers that it is empty except for chalk, she snorts.

"I'll bring you another apple soon," I say when I can find my words. "And I'll collect colors to protect you. I won't let the Black Horse get you. I promise."

Slowly, slowly, I lift my bare hand.

I bring it down on her muzzle. A single touch. I feel her velvet coat, her gentle warmth. She is so powerful. And then she tosses her head and prances off to her corner of the garden and watches me.

I smile.

It is a start.

I flip over the letter, and write on the back:

Dear Horse Lord,

I was afraid that I'd forgotten all the colors of the rainbow, but I know just where I can find them again. You can count on me.

Truly,
Emmaline May

16

ANNA'S COLORED PENCILS were a gift from Dr. Turner.

Anna has been at Briar Hill longer than any of the rest of us. She came two years ago on the first trains rumbling through the countryside. She brought two beaten-up suitcases with her. One was full of winter coats and stockings that her mother had packed. The other was full of naturalist books—that one she had packed herself. Sister Constance said Anna used to like to wander the gardens, like me, long before they were eaten by ivy. She would sit on a bench and read and read and read amid the spring flowers. But then the stillwaters got worse with the summer rains, and by August she was bedridden. She couldn't see the flowers anymore. Dr. Turner brought her the pencils so she could draw them. I don't think anyone has ever told her that all the flowers have long since died.

I knock on her door.

"Come in."

Her voice is tired.

I push open the door, and she smiles and pats the bed, but I don't climb up. There is a handkerchief in her hand that is primly folded, mostly hidden in her palm, and I wonder if there is blood inside. She has the mirror on her nightstand tilted away from her face. In its reflection, I can just make out winged horses beyond the mirror-window, grazing in the dead grass, with their wings folded tightly against the wind.

"May I see your colored pencils?" I ask.

At first, I had thought to use the pencils for the spectral shield. But I could never take Anna's beloved pencils away from her, not even to save Foxfire. And besides, the Horse Lord said the objects had to be large enough to be seen from a distance. But they can still help me remember the colors of the rainbow. They can be my guide.

Anna leans forward to open the secret desk drawer, and the motion stirs the stillwaters. Murkiness rises in her lungs, and she muffles a cough. She takes out the box of colored pencils and some paper, but I shake my head.

"I don't need paper."

She gives me a curious look, but doesn't ask. She sets the

The winged horses are stirring.

box on the bed. Anna is nothing if not organized, and the eight pencils are arranged just as the manufacturer boxed them, a spectrum of rainbow colors.

845-CARMINE RED

848-BLUSH PINK

849-TANGERINE ORANGE

863-CANARY YELLOW

865-EMERALD GREEN

867-SEA TURQUOISE

868-LAPIS BLUE

876-HELIOTROPE PURPLE

I press my finger into the tips of each pencil that Anna keeps so carefully sharpened.

"What's wrong, Emmaline? You look unhappy."

"I need to borrow them."

It is Anna's turn to look displeased. "We've talked about this. You can have paper and chalk, and you can use the pencils here in my room anytime you want, but they are too dear to me. I'm sorry, you can't take them with you."

The Horse Lord's letter is stiff in my pocket. I run my finger over the paper's edge again and again. My eyes shift to the mirror on her side table. The winged horses are stirring. The winds are growing stronger on the other side of the mirror, sweeping their manes and long tangled tails into their eyes. One in front, a dark brown horse with a bald face, throws its head toward the sky as if sensing danger. If I tell Anna how dire Foxfire's situation is, she might try to go outside again. And I am afraid of how thin her arms look. Afraid of what more snow would do to her.

"Why can't you just draw with them here, like you usually do?" She motions to the fan of drawings laid out on her bed.

I slip my hand out of my pocket.

"It's a secret."

"Does this have to do with the winged horse in the sundial garden?"

I pause. "Her name is Foxfire."

Anna's eyes, for just a second, flick to the mirror. Inside it, the horses are starting to run now. Faster and faster, racing the wind, across the front lawn. They're almost to the stone fence that separates the hospital grounds from Mr. Mason's farm. The horse in front stretches out its white-tipped wings at the last minute and soars. Does Anna see the horses? Does she see them fly?

But no. She is only looking at the dried lavender next to the mirror. Sister Constance says the smell is good for the stillwaters, but I think it must be the shape of the flower that Anna likes best, because she draws it over and over.

Anna runs her fingers over the box of pencils. "Well, it sounds very important, so you may borrow one at a time," she says. "Which would you like first?"

I point to *863-CANARY YELLOW*. The color of Marjorie's

raincoat. Anna draws it out of the box with fingers that are so fragile and so white that they could almost be bone china.

I study the pencil. I think of all the things that are yellow in the hospital. Butter. Sweet corn. Tinned peaches. My stomach grumbles. It's almost teatime. The smell of broth is coming from downstairs, and then Sister Mary Grace walks in with a tray of leek stew and a glass of water for Anna.

"Emmaline," Sister Mary Grace says, "go round up the little ones and tell them tea is nearly ready."

I slip the yellow pencil in my pocket next to the Horse Lord's curled note. I couldn't put butter or sweet corn or peaches in the sundial garden. Foxfire would just eat them.

I go to the library, and to the ballroom filled with wooden benches to make a chapel, and finally find the three little mice and Arthur outside, sitting on the kitchen stairs.

"It's teatime," I say. They jump at my voice and then giggle in their mouse language, which poor mute Arthur must not understand, because he starts sucking his thumb. He stares at me with his big wide eyes, and then looks past me at the tin laundry tub, and then Beth pokes him and they all scamper past, into the kitchen. I grab hold of Susan, the littlest mouse.

"Where exactly did you find those long black feathers you had the other day?" I ask.

"Right there," she says proudly, pointing to the corner of the terrace where Sister Mary Grace does our laundry. "They blew off the roof, I think. When the snow melts, I bet we'll find hundreds of them. Kitty says they must come from giant crows that have flown all the way from America."

I let her go, and she flounces back to the others, who are waiting.

I look toward the roof.

I do not think that there are crows that big anywhere, not even in America.

And then I take a step toward the far edge of the terrace, where laundry basins are stacked, and go no farther, in case one of the Sisters is watching from a window.

My foot squishes in something wet and smelly.

Cripes.

Sheep droppings. I drag my boot across the bricks to wipe the muck off, but pause. Something isn't right. There are small bones of tiny animals in the clumps. Bird wings and mouse teeth. Things that shouldn't be in manure at all. Perhaps these droppings are from foxes. Or perhaps they are from a wicked horse that hunts other animals, a horse that leaves angry hoof prints on the roof and rains down long black feathers. I smell a trace of rotting seaweed.

I jerk upright, feeling queasy.

I hurry back into the hospital and slam the kitchen

door, heart racing fast. Even through layers of stone and wood and slate tiles, I can feel the Black Horse circling overhead. Foxfire may be safe now, but each night the moon will grow brighter. Before long, the Black Horse will see her, and she will not be able to fly away.

I need to find something yellow. *Soon.*

17

DR. TURNER PRESSES the silver stethoscope to my back.

I can see his face in the mirror. He is frowning. Woolly-worm eyebrows knit together. Mustached mouth pinched. He lowers the stethoscope around his neck and lets out a sigh, but when he turns to me the frown is gone. He dissolves two fat aspirin tablets in water and hands me the glass.

"Gargle this and count to twenty, then spit."

I count slowly in my head, and then spit into a mug. When I look up, he is holding a yellow ticket. His eyes are not quite on mine. He clears his throat. "And affix this outside your door."

I stare at the ticket.

Yellow?

The Sisters and Dr. Turner think we do not know what the tickets mean, but of course we do. Of course. Yellow means extra doses of cod liver oil. Yellow means only feeling the sunlight from a window.

Yellow means red is one step away.

"You're wrong," I say, and my voice is hard. "I'm getting better. I'm not like the really ill children. I only cough sometimes. I'd like the blue ticket, please."

He does not give me the blue. He does not say anything. His eyebrows go extra woolly, and he turns away to write notes in his book.

My voice rises unsteadily. "Can I at least have a chocolate?"

His pencil stops, and he takes a deep breath, and then keeps writing. He sighs deeply. "There are no more chocolates."

I shove the ticket into my pocket, beneath an apple I brought to give Foxfire later. While Dr. Turner writes, I watch the winged horses in the mirror-room, but I am too stunned to laugh when they bump the edges of the butler's pantry, sniffing around the mirror-medicine bottles, nosing through Dr. Turner's mirror-medical bag. One accidentally knocks over a box of tongue depressors and it clatters to the floor, and the horses jerk up in surprise and race each other for the doorway.

I turn away from them. On our side of the mirror, the real box of tongue depressors still sits on the sideboard.

Then I see it: the label on Dr. Turner's big bottle of aspirin. It is yellow—*863*-CANARY YELLOW—the exact match to Anna's colored pencil in my pocket. The label is old and peeling at the edges, but what matters is the bright, bright color, so bright it will hurt the Black Horse's eyes.

Dr. Turner mumbles to himself and turns to the cabinet to write something on his pad of paper.

I glance at the bottle. I could take it. Now, while his back is turned.

In the mirror, one of the winged horses has stuck its head through the door once more, watching me.

Now.

I grab the bottle and try to peel off the yellow label, but it sticks. I'll have to take the whole bottle. There are only two pills left in it. Two pills cannot save Anna's life. Two pills cannot stop Kitty's cough. But that yellow label might help Foxfire. My heart pounds, pounds, and something stirs in the stillwaters. I stash the bottle in my pocket just as Dr. Turner turns around, and the stillwaters flood my lungs, and my whole body shakes.

He reaches for a fresh handkerchief. "You must remember to cover your mouth when you cough. It's very important."

How can I remember to do anything at all, with a yellow ticket burning a hole in my pocket? I slide off the examination table. It isn't until I open the back door to the terrace and breathe fresh air that my lungs start to calm.

The sound of clanking pots comes from the opened kitchen window. I don't have much time before Sister Mary Grace will come find me to peel potatoes. She'll take one look at the yellow ticket and tell me I can't go outside anymore, not even to the terrace.

I dart to the garden wall, and climb it.

When the snows first fell, and the world was pristine and white, Foxfire blended into it as if she were made of snow herself. But the snow is not pristine anymore. It's muddy with earth. Dirty snow coats Foxfire's legs and underbelly. When she tosses her head, her mane falls in thick clumps that are in need of a good combing. Winter-dead sticks tangle in her tail.

But my heart still soars when I see her.

"You are a mess," I say. Then I realize my own hair is just as tangled, my own boots caked in mud. "Well, *we* are a mess."

Foxfire tosses her head as though she agrees. She comes right up and noses at my pocket until I take out the apple. She chomps at it before I can even lay my palm flat.

Hesitantly, not sure if I've earned her full trust yet, I reach up to her mane. "Easy there. I'm just going to untangle these sticks."

She stops mid-bite, eyes swiveling toward my hand, but she doesn't buck or rear. I am close. So close. And then my hand is on her neck. *Oh,* she feels alive. Her white hair is caked in cold clumps of mud, but there is warmth underneath. I can almost feel her heart fluttering. Can she feel mine, too?

"That's lovely. See? That's nice."

Slowly, I stroke her neck from ear to shoulder, ear to shoulder, and bits of crumbly mud and dust rain down to the ground and make me cough. She seems to calm with each stroke. I free all the twigs I can, but the dirt goes deep. I will have to ask Thomas if he has a comb.

I leave her and take the pill bottle out and search through the wall of ivy near the red ribbon until I find a vine just the right size, and tuck the bottle into it. The bottle's yellow label looks even more yellow, like the first sunshine crocuses that peek out after a long winter. My mother used to scold Marjorie when she would pick those flowers, but Marjorie did anyway. She would press them between the pages of Mama's fattest recipe book until they were thin as tissue, and then frame them above her bed, so that it would always be spring.

In my pocket, Dr. Turner's yellow ticket rustles. Foxfire watches as I take it out and quietly tear it into pieces, and then bury them under the snow.

A cloud passes overhead, casting the garden into shadows, and we look up. We are thinking the same thing: You never know where the Black Horse might be lurking. Behind the twisting winter-dead branches of the old oaks in front of the hospital; behind the low-sitting clouds; just waiting for a sliver of moonlight, when he can resume his hunt.

"Do you think the Black Horse can see that bottle from way up high?"

Foxfire moves her head in a way that could be a nod, or a shake, or a shrug, then goes to stand in the corner of the garden that gets the most sun. The light cuts her body in two. Half in light, half in shadow.

She snorts.

I look back up at the sky. The clouds have moved, and the sun shines right onto the bottle. It makes the glass glow and the label gleam. "Yes," I say. "Yes, in the full moon, I think that will burn the eyes right out of his head."

18

KNOCK, KNOCK.

"Come in," Thomas calls from the other side of the barn door. I peek inside. He is mucking out the pen into a wheelbarrow. Bog is curled on the barn's dirt floor next to the stack of pine boxes. His face breaks in one of those smiling-dog pants.

I step all the way inside and let my eyes wander over the barn. The barn is Thomas's domain. A place of men, and animals, and tools with sharp points. But it smells nice in here, like the hay in my straw mattress, and like sweet oats. A gas mask hangs on the back of the workbench, half forgotten. I fiddle with the rubber strap.

"I was looking for a comb for Foxfire."

He pauses, wiping his bare hand over his forehead. Do

the Americans knit special mittens for one-handed boys, I wonder?

"Do you know how to groom a horse?" he asks, curious.

I try not to look too long at his empty sleeve fastened with a diaper pin. I bend down to scratch Bog's head. He rolls over and sticks one leg in the air so I can rub his belly with the tip of my boot. The action makes his whole body move up and down, up and down.

"Because I could show you, if you don't," Thomas continues. "Picking out the hooves can be tricky." He digs through his bin of old brushes and combs until he finds a hoof pick, and hands it to me.

"And then there's combing out the mane." He holds up a wide comb with thin metal bristles. "You have to start at the ends and work your way up." He gestures in the air with the comb. "Same with the tail. As far as the wings, leave them alone, I think, if she's wounded. Best to let these things heal in their own time. . . ."

He trails off as footsteps approach outside.

Knock, knock.

Quick and almost apologetic. Thomas and I exchange a look. He sets aside the comb and opens the door. Sister Mary Grace is there. She jumps a little when he pushes the door wide.

"Sister?"

"Thomas. Men are here to see you." She pauses. "Officers."

She pulls on the sleeves of her black nun's habit as though even with yards and yards of fabric, it is still not enough material to hide behind. Her eyes shift to me and Bog. "Emmaline? What are you . . ." She sighs. "Go on back inside. Quick feet."

Thomas whistles for Bog, who is on all fours in a flash, pressed to his heels.

I trudge back with them to the house. Sister Mary Grace rests a hand on my shoulder, rubbing the short tufts of my hair. Sister Constance's pinched face peers through the glass windowpanes in the door, and then the door swings open for us. There are two men with her. They are young, with crisp uniforms and black hair beneath their caps.

Sister Constance gives me a stern look. "You know you aren't to go out now that you have a yellow ticket, Emmaline. Especially not as far as the barn."

"I'm sorry, Sister. I won't sneak around anymore, I promise."

"Indeed." Her voice is hard.

She closes the door in Bog's face before he can come in. He presses his dog-nose to the glass panes in the door, fogging it. Thomas starts to say something, but then stops. The soldiers seem young and affable, like they could be friends of his, but they do not smile.

"Mr. Thomas Whatley?"

"That's me, yes."

I watch over my shoulder as I drift down the hall,

moving as slowly as I can. When I reach the library, it is filled with whispers. How odd. I go inside, where Benny and Jack and ten other children who are supposed to be preparing for class are pressed against the wall.

"What are you—"

"Quiet, flea!" Jack says in a scowling whisper. "We can hear, if you shut your mouth."

I scowl back at him. His Lionel steam engine toy train with the real working whistle sits beside him; I'm tempted to kick it. Send the hunk of shiny green metal across the floor—

My breath catches.

Green.

The train's paint glimmers in the light: 865-EMERALD GREEN. It would serve him right, Benny's little stoolie, if the train disappeared. . . .

Muffled soldiers' voices come from down the hallway. Beth, one of the three little mice, scoots over and taps the floor next to her. Tearing my eyes away from Jack's train, I press into the warm bodies of feverish children, my ear to the thin wall. I can only make out every few words in the soldiers' soft voices. Something about a battle somewhere near Egypt. A shell and a hospital. Then Thomas lets out a single sharp moan.

"What's happened?" Susan, the littlest mouse, who has just come in, whispers. "Is it about the war?"

"Of course it's about the war," Benny snaps. "It's always about the war, if it's soldiers. They're talking about Thomas's father. He was off fighting Rommel's men in the western desert campaign. I think he's been killed." Benny tiptoes to the library door and peeks around in the hall. After a moment he comes back, and he makes a big gesture of taking off his cap, just as the soldier did. "They handed Thomas a package. I think it was his father's last belongings from the hospital, paperwork and things. They said something about medals of honor, too, and gave him a little box stamped with the king's own crest. Said his father was one of England's finest heroes."

"Poor Thomas," Susan says.

Benny holds his chin high. "Such things happen. We must carry on."

Peter coughs.

Sister Mary Grace sticks her head in the library and hisses that they can hear us whispering down the hall. We all scramble to our feet and rush out of the library, and there's the sound of feet running upstairs and then doors slamming up and down the residence hall.

I pause and look back toward the library once more; Jack's train is gone. He must have taken it with him.

"What's happened?" Anna is calling from her bedroom upstairs. "Hello? Won't someone tell me?"

But no one answers her.

By the front door, the soldiers are still talking quietly to Thomas, who is clutching a package filled with papers and things in his long arm. Sister Mary Grace has one of her hands over her mouth. Thomas has his back to me. His shoulders sag. I cannot see his face.

Slowly, I climb the stairs all the way to my attic room. I feel hot tears on my cheeks. Thomas is not a monster, I am certain of it. And he is hurting.

I push open the frosted window. If I lean out, I can see the corner of the walled gardens.

I know that the red ribbon and the yellow bottle are there, tucked safely into the ivy. Soon, I hope, I can add a snotty boy's emerald green Lionel steam engine with a working whistle to the spectral shield.

I peer upward, just in case. The skies are clear. No Black Horse circling, though I know he is near. Waiting. Smelling. Hunting.

Down below, on the front steps, Bog sits in the cold, face against the glass, waiting for Thomas.

19

THE OLD PRINCESS LIKED to collect things. I know this because my room is in the attic. And except for that one time Jack and Benny sneaked up for a smoke, I am the only child who ever comes here. The stairs are narrow and steep. There are no lights, except for candles and lanterns, and a single window at each end. The storerooms are dusty and filled with crates covered in spiderwebs and stamped with words in foreign languages. Most of the crates are empty. When the princess left, she took almost everything valuable from downstairs, except the china plates and things we might need in the hospital. But I think, in her old age, she forgot about the boxes up here. I think everyone forgot.

It is lights-out, and I promised Sister Constance I wouldn't sneak around, but in the attic I can move unseen and unheard. I light a candle and put it on a plate, which I set down next to the biggest box, an old trunk with rotting leather straps and sea-salt stains in the corners.

Outside, beyond the window, the moon is already a sliver, and it will grow more each night. I think of the box of Anna's pencils. So many colors to find, and so far I have only two.

The trunk's lid is heavier than I expected, and I strain to lift it off and lower it so it doesn't crash loudly. It is packed with straw that is so old it has turned to dust. It catches in my throat and I stifle a cough as I dig around and find a package wrapped in newsprint. I unwrap it to find a small carving of a frog. It's lovely, but made of gray stone, and the last thing I need is anything else gray, so I place it back in the crate. I unwrap another object: a golden box with a beetle on top and little pictures and symbols drawn on the sides. I'm not sure if gold counts as a proper color, since it isn't on the pencil manufacturer's list of rainbow colors. I don't like the beetle anyway, so back into the trunk it goes. Then I pull out a velvet bag filled with clinking trinkets, and roll them onto my palm. Loose stone beads and some small carvings to go on a necklace: a woman with wings and a creature with a man's body but a dog's head. And *then*. A long string of blue-green beads that sparkle in the lantern light, and for the briefest moment, I do feel like a real explorer.

867-SEA TURQUOISE.

The color matches Anna's turquoise colored pencil exactly! I carefully place the turquoise beads in my pocket and stand, dusting off my nightgown. Beside the heavy trunk are smaller boxes from a millinery. Some are round, some are long and flat, with LOCK & CO. and EDE & RAVENSCROFT stamped on the side. In the first one, I find an old-fashioned black hat with a short veil. The second and third are empty except for miles and miles of tissue paper. When I open the last one, my eyes light up. It is filled with soft satin fabric. *848*-BLUSH PINK! I grin in delight at my good fortune and tear through the crumpled tissue paper to snatch it up. Only—it is not just fabric. It is a garment, and there is lace on the edges, and as I hold it up to the light, my eyes go wide.

It is a nightgown.

Not like my nightgown. Like one of *those* nightgowns. A *woman's* nightgown.

Did this belong to the old princess? I can't imagine a proper, distinguished lady dressed in pink silk and lace. I giggle a little at the thought, and then cover my mouth.

I should leave it in the box. I can't go stringing up ladies' underwear on the garden wall. What if Thomas peeks into the garden? What if the Horse Lord himself sees it, while delivering one of his notes?

But pink is not a common color. There is no powdered

blush here. There are no sweetheart boxes of chocolates. So I fold the nightgown and gather the string of beads. Four colors now, and four to go. And then my cheeks go warm. I think about that old princess dancing around in her fancy pink nightgown, and I laugh out loud, before pressing a hand once more to my mouth, and then stifling a cough.

20

"OH, POOR THOMAS! You should have told me straightaway."

Anna is cross with me. I give her back the yellow colored pencil, hoping it will make her feel better. She sighs, her eyes red, as she places the box back in its proper spot and lays it on her bed, next to the open book of *Flora and Fauna.*

I pick up the box and run my fingers over the sharpened pencils' tips. *865-*EMERALD GREEN. Other than Jack's train, what else matches this color? Pine needles would only turn brown. There's the faded sofa in the library, but I'd need four grown men to lift it.

It has to be the train.

"Was Thomas's father quite famous?" I ask.

"He was well decorated, yes. He even received the Victoria Cross. Back during the Great War, when he was Thomas's age, he was a private in the cavalry, and during the Battle of Cambrai they say he rode so fast he was able to warn every man in the trenches about encroaching gas. That was before they mechanized everything. In this war, they promoted him to sergeant and assigned him to the Special Air Service. There are newspaper articles about him and everything, you know; Thomas keeps a scrapbook. His aunt in Wales started sending him the clippings, after his mother died." She sighs again and looks down at her hands. "He wasn't exactly acknowledged by his father."

"Why?"

Her cheeks flush. "He couldn't be a soldier because of his arm."

"What will he do now?"

"The same as the rest of us. Stay here. Tend to the sheep. Eat rotting onions and wait."

I replace the green pencil in the box. "Do you think he can pick a horse's hoof with just one hand?"

Anna raises an eyebrow. "Why do you ask?"

I shrug.

She looks wistfully toward the ceiling and presses a hand against the base of her throat. "I think Thomas can do anything. I think if they'd just have put a gun in his hand, he'd have won this war."

I roll over onto my back and look at Anna's ceiling.

This was the princess's own bedroom, once. The ceiling is covered with an oil painting of Greek gods, some strong and handsome, others with fat little bellies and curls cut from stone. She tells me stories about them. Zeus. Hera. Hades. But only when the Sisters aren't nearby. They call those stories *blasphemous*.

"Do you miss your family?" Anna asks suddenly.

I take out the blue colored pencil. No. The red. Some things are red in the hospital. Anna's felt hat. The soup cans in the kitchen pantry. But I already have the Horse Lord's red ribbon.

"Emmaline?"

I replace the red colored pencil. "I miss my horses."

She settles back into her pillows, gazing out the window, running her fingers lovingly along her book's spine. "You'll see them again."

"No. I won't." I think of Thomas's father, and I picture my horses, and my mouth is filling with ash, and I swallow it down, and down, but it keeps coming up. "They're dead."

Her head snaps to me. "Oh, little goose. I'm so sorry."

I think of the horses kicking and kicking at their stalls, and no one to let them out.

"The stories of the bombings were just awful," she says. "Everyone talks about London, but Nottingham got it bad too, didn't it? So many souls lost, in just one night. And all the fires. I heard they still found some fires smoldering even after a week, when they went through the rubble looking for ... people." She pauses. "Do you want to talk about it, Em?"

I take out the purple pencil and hold it up to the light.

Anna reaches out and strokes my short tufts of hair. "Of course you don't. You'd have to be mad to want to think about that sort of thing. Much better to think about when we go home and see our families again. I'm going to hug them all, especially my brother, Sam. He's going to make it through the war, I know it."

She tilts her book in my direction. "I've decided that I'm going to study to be a professor of natural sciences. I did some research on the name of your winged horse, Fox-fire, and I discovered the most magnificent thing." She flips the page and points to an illustration of a glowing insect. "Did you know there are creatures that glow? It's a phenomenon that happens in certain insects and fungi and sea creatures." She traces a hand down the page, lovingly. "Before people knew what caused it, they thought it was magic. They called it will-o'-the-wisp, and fairy fire, and honey glow." She smiles. "Fox fire, too."

"Foxfire is named after glowing *bugs*?"

"Fox fire is a type of glowing plant," she clarifies with a laugh. "As logs decompose, a bioluminescent fungus grows within and casts a blue light. In some cases, it's bright enough to read by at night."

I stare at the illustrations in her book.

"I was thinking that when you're an explorer and travel

the world, you could find fox fire on your own. The biolu-
minescence, I mean—not the horse. Darwin wrote about
it once: 'While sailing in these latitudes on one very dark
night, the sea presented a wonderful and most beautiful
spectacle. Every part of the surface glowed with a pale
light.'" She smiles. "Maybe you'll discover a new species,
and name it *Mycena emmaline,* or *Mycena marjorie.* Wouldn't
your sister be tickled to have a fungus named after her?"

I push off from the bed. The mirror over Anna's
dresser is quiet. The winged horses are gone now, and it
seems so empty over there, with just the mirror-me and the
mirror-her.

"Emmaline?"

I walk out the door silently and wander down the long
hallway. All the rooms are quiet, except for the last one,
where little Arthur is snoring on his bed. There is a curio
cabinet in an alcove filled with simple things that the old
princess didn't bother to take with her: Bird nests. Snake
skins. A carved rock. Things someone probably found on
the grounds. I open the glass cabinet and pick up a stack of
yellowing old calling cards in a chipped fruit dish. *Professor
H. K. Hopper, Egyptologist. Lord Barchester. Miss A. Rodan, Aviatrix.*

These must be all the famous people who came to visit
the old princess, whose treasures, gifts for Her Highness,
are stored in the attic. I wonder if Thomas's father ever
came.

I glance back in the direction of Anna's room.

She told me I could be an explorer—someone famous, just like the people on these cards. She told me I already *am*.

I wonder sometimes if Anna understands me better than anyone else in the world.

I smile. Just a little, just to myself.

21

WHISPERS COME FROM DOWN THE HALL.

I stuff the cards back into the fruit dish and hurry to close the curio case. Following the voices, I come upon the library. Rodger, the boy with the port-wine birthmark, and Susan are working on sums for Sister Constance's maths class at the study table. Their backs are to me. Jack is asleep on the sofa not far from them. On the rug beside him, three inches from his hand, is his Lionel steam engine.

I dare a glance down the hall; it's empty. I could take the train. A famous explorer wouldn't shy away from an important mission, and neither will I.

Now.

I drop to hands and knees, keeping low so the other children don't see me. Elbow over elbow, knee over knee, I crawl through the no-man's-land of the library floor. Jack mumbles in his sleep and tosses his hand down. His fingers graze the train and I go rigid. The other children stop whispering for a moment. My heart goes *rat-a-tat, rat-a-tat,* and I dare a glance up at enemy territory. Still facing away from me.

The train is close, but his crumb-covered fingers are on it.

Drawing in a sharp breath, I crawl forward with all the silence of the best of Britain's spies. I delicately take hold of the end of the train—being careful not to touch the real working whistle—and pull it away. Inch by inch. The wheels roll silently across the rug, until Jack's fingers slip off of it.

I go still, heart pounding.

But he doesn't wake.

And then I'm fleeing the battlefield, train tucked under one arm, into the safety of the hall. Footsteps are coming—*trapped!* I spy the curio cabinet across from me and hide the train far back on the bottom shelf, behind a soft fox's pelt, just as Sister Constance turns the corner.

I freeze.

Her lips press together firmly—it was only yesterday that I promised Sister Constance not to sneak around. "Emmaline!" She darts forward and grabs my ear. "You are supposed to be in quiet study in the library, young lady."

"*Ow, ow, ow,*" I plead, but she pulls me a few feet down the hall, then lets me go.

"Go to your room for the remainder of the day, and ask God for forgiveness for your disobedience. If I see the slightest glimpse of you before breakfast tomorrow, I'll put a bell around your neck like a cat."

I head for the stairs, head hung low, but heart still secretly thrilled as I think of the hidden train. The chapel door is near the stairs, and I pause, because candles are glowing from within, even though it isn't Sunday. The altar is draped in heavy liturgical cloth, presiding over three rows of wooden benches. Someone is sitting on the first bench, mouth moving in quiet prayer.

Thomas.

He reaches out and touches the altar cloth. It is a rich, royal purple reserved for Advent and Lent. The same shade as Anna's colored pencil. *876*-HELIOTROPE PURPLE.

Thomas lets his hand fall away from the cloth. He's still whispering, though the words are too quiet to make out.

From somewhere deep in my chest, the stillwaters stir. They swell, prickling at the inside of my lungs, until I feel heavy and drowned, like I've fallen off Darwin's ship into the sea of sparkling little creatures.

"Emmaline," Sister Constance calls sternly. She points toward the attic stairs. *"Now."*

I climb, thoughts jumping between Thomas and his

father, the toy train and the purple altar cloth and Sister Constance, but at the top of the stairs, my eyes settle on my door, and I go still.

A sudden burst of anger surges inside of me.

A yellow ticket! Someone has replaced the one I tore up! I leap up to rip it off, but then I remember Dr. Turner has a whole stack of them. If I take it down, he will only replace it with another.

I throw myself on top of my bed, not touching my books or my schoolwork.

There is no point. There will always be Sister Constance watching. There will always be a yellow ticket. I will never be a proper explorer. I will never see the pyramids of Egypt. I will never watch the wild horses running free on the plains of America. I will never discover anything at all, except dust.

But *no.*

I sit up.

Anna believes in me, and Anna is the smartest person I know.

I snatch up some chalk and write on the back of one of my old drawings:

Dear Horse Lord,

I do not know if this letter will reach you, but I need you to know that I won't give up, not ever. I have already found five colorful objects to protect Foxfire: a red one, a yellow one, a

*turquoise one, a pink one, and now a green one. I am working
as fast as I can before the full moon comes to find the rest, but
I have an important question: Do you think God will be angry
with me if I steal the purple liturgical cloth from the chapel?*

Truly,
Emmaline May

I think of the calling card in the curio cabinet belonging to *Miss A. Rodan, Aviatrix,* and I fold the drawing in half, and in half again, and then fold down the corners.

An airplane.

I push open the window and lean into the wind.

I cast out the paper airplane, whispering prayers as it flies, flies, flies toward the gardens, hoping that it lands true.

22

THE NEXT DAY IS SUNDAY.

Sunday is the day we eat leftover bread for breakfast, both to remember Christ's fasting and because it is Thomas's day off and the Sisters have to tend to the sheep after they tend to us at Mass. Though there are three benches, Sister Constance says we must crowd into the front two to be closer to God and his healing powers.

Benny sits in the row behind me and kicks me in the backside.

I ignore him and look at the ceiling. It is covered with black cloths. Anna told me that when she first arrived, the ceiling was decorated with a beautiful Greek painting like the one in her bedroom. The old princess had brought over real Greek painters and everything, but the Sisters of Mercy forbade pagan idolatry in a chapel, even if it did used to be a ballroom.

As Sister Constance reads from the Bible, I imagine all the beautiful couples who once danced here. I bet the ladies wore dresses that were all the colors of the rainbow, and the men had top hats and dashing mustaches. They would twirl and twirl in the candlelight, beneath the ancient floating gods who drink wine and ride wild stallions. I wonder if the horses lived in the mirrors even back then. Maybe that is why the princess stayed here for so long, by herself. Maybe she liked waking up each morning and seeing a winged horse in her bedroom mirror. Maybe she found a way to talk to them. Maybe—just maybe—she met the Horse Lord.

Sister Constance ends the prayer, and we stand, and someone taps my shoulder.

I turn around to find Thomas.

He clears his throat and reaches into his pocket. "Bog chased a rabbit into the old gardens this morning," he says. "There's a hole in the rear gate. When he came back he had this tangled in his fur, along with a mess of briars. You're the only one who ever goes in those gardens, so I thought it must be meant for you."

He takes out a slightly crumpled, damp letter tied in red ribbon.

I silence a gasp as I cram the letter into my sleeve, looking left and right to make sure the other children haven't seen.

"It is for me," I whisper quickly.

I eye him closely, wondering if he sneaked a peek at the Horse Lord's letter, but the knot is tied firmly, the red ribbon only slightly torn. The Horse Lord must have left this for me in the sundial, where last night's wind blew it into the briars.

I give him a solemn nod. "Thank you."

He nods solemnly back.

After the service, the other children go to their rooms to quietly read the Bible and pray, but I tiptoe back up the stairs and past the shut doors on the residence hall to a closet where I can read the Horse Lord's letter. I can hardly believe that my airplane reached him. The paper is damp, and the handwriting is strangely shaky, as though he was very tired while writing.

Dear Emmaline May,

I found your note in a rosebush near the sundial, folded curiously. To answer your question, I would never condone stealing, not even in the name of a higher deed. I suggest that you only borrow the liturgical cloth. Perhaps after church services conclude, so it will not be missed for a full week. By then, with luck, Foxfire's wing will have healed and you can return it safe and sound without anyone else's knowledge. That God will see you, I have

no doubt. But that God will know what is deeper within your
heart, I am also certain.

Ride true,
The Horse Lord

I stash the letter back in my sleeve.

The Horse Lord is so wise—*now* is the time to borrow the cloth, long before it'll be used again. But can I
really steal it from God? I suppose I don't have a choice.
I've scoured the hospital, and this is the only purple object,
except for the stained glass in the windows, and that isn't
coming out.

I exhale slowly. I can do this.

I tiptoe out of the closet and into the hallway. Voices
come from the room Benny and Jack and Peter share, and
I pause. I've always wondered if Benny really prays on Sunday afternoons. When I peek through the keyhole, all three
boys are sitting cross-legged on Peter's bed, Peter and Jack
staring in rapt attention as Benny reads to them.

"'Unhand me, you brute! Popeye! Popeye, save me!'"

Not the Bible.

I sneak upstairs to grab my coat and the other colorful
objects I've found, and then tiptoe back down the stairs
and hold my breath when I pass Sister Constance's office,
where she is digging through stacks of newspapers with
loud headlines.

I continue down the hall to the empty chapel and close

the door behind me. The air is still warm from the twenty bodies that were here earlier. The altar is bare. Sister Mary Grace must have already pressed and folded the liturgical cloth to use next week. I tiptoe to the closet where they lock up the cloth, along with the sacred wine and gold cross, but I've seen them hang the key on a hook in the back. I stand on my tiptoes to reach it.

Inside the closet, I find the Advent cloth. I run my hand over the purple fabric.

I wonder: Is this a sin?

And then I think: This is most definitely a sin.

My lungs are feeling heavy. It is difficult to draw anything but a shallow breath. But I fight past the feeling, and snatch the altar cloth. It slips like silk beneath my fingers as I ball it up and stash it under my coat, and then slam the closet door. The rest of the objects—the nightgown, engine, and beads—weigh down my pockets.

"Emmaline?"

Sister Mary Grace, in the chapel doorway, peers at me curiously. She is wearing heavy men's boots that are caked in dried mud, and there is a bucket of sheep's milk in one hand. "What are you doing in here?"

I know now why foxes sometimes freeze when the hunting dogs chase them. It is because any direction they run might be the wrong one. "I just . . ." I gape. "I was just . . . praying."

She raises an eyebrow. "With your coat on?"

I swallow hard, thinking. "I couldn't find my sweater and I was cold."

"Well." She seems a bit uncertain, but the pail is getting heavy in her hand. "Praying is . . . good. But you should do so in your room. You don't want Sister Constance to catch you out and about."

She goes down the hallway, casting one last look over her shoulder. Once she turns the corner, I scramble through the library window and then take off across the field to the gardens. Bog barks from the barn, but I shush him and keep running, and then scale up the ivy. It's hard to climb with just one arm, the other one holding the cloth so it doesn't get snagged. But I manage, and drop down on the other side.

Foxfire swivels her head at me.

"I hope you're grateful for this," I say. "I was nearly caught." But looking at her, I know it was worth it.

I shake out the beautiful purple cloth. In the sunlight, it shines even brighter. Foxfire seems taken with it, and she comes closer through the mud to inspect it. I take off my mittens and tie the cloth's corners carefully to the ivy, making sure it doesn't drape in the mud. Next to the red ribbon and the yellow bottle, I string up the turquoise necklace and the green toy train and, blushing, the ladies' nightgown. This has officially become the most colorful corner of the hospital grounds.

I reach out and pat Foxfire on the nose, then nuzzle my

own nose into her neck and breathe in her horse smell. "See? Your wing looks better already. It'll be healed in plenty of time for me to get this cloth back by next Sunday."

I write the Horse Lord another note.

Dear Horse Lord,

It worked! At this rate, Foxfire is going to be safe until she is a creaky old knock-kneed mare—how long do winged horses live, anyway? I am only missing two colors now, blue and orange. I've hung up all the other objects, even the pink ladies' nightgown. (Which was embarrassing!)

Truly,
Emmaline May

Post script: Your handwriting was shaky in your letter. I hope nothing is the matter. Please write back.

I start to climb back up the ivy, but something tugs at my coat. Foxfire, nipping at the hem. I drop back down. She stamps her hoof, impatiently.

"I don't have any more apples. I'm sorry."

She stamps her hoof again, and then noses at my shoulder, hard enough to push me back against the ivy. The air whooshes out of me.

"Hey, watch it, I—"

She noses me again, harder. It truly hurts this time. The Horse Lord needs to teach his horse some manners! I'm about to give her a good shove, when a shadow passes over the garden. *Whoosh.* At first I think it's just another cloud crossing the sun's path. But it flickers. It has wings stretched far like an airplane, but then the wings pull in, and draw out again.

I tilt my head toward the sky, filled with dread. The shadow is gone now, but Foxfire and I both know what it was.

23

THE BLACK HORSE.

I turn to Foxfire with a gasp. "You were trying to warn me, weren't you?"

She noses me again toward the wall of ivy. She is a smart horse. She knows that is how I can get to safety—but I shake my head.

"I'm not going to leave you." I pull her closer against the wall, and raise the corner of the altar cloth to hide us both under. I know the Black Horse can't see us because it is daylight, but he can still smell. The altar cloth holds the church's scent of incense, and, with luck, it is enough to mask our own. I wrap my arms midway around Foxfire's neck and close my eyes. Our warm breaths mix together beneath the tent of the altar cloth.

Is he there, flying overhead?

But then, footsteps sound on the other side of the garden wall. Maybe it is Thomas, walking through the fallen leaves. But no, it is Thomas's day off, and after church he goes to Wick.

"Bog?" I whisper desperately. "Is that you?"

There is no answer at first.

Then: *Clomp. Clomp.*

My heart thunders once, twice, three times. It's the Black Horse! He's on the ground! I did not think he would come for us in the day. I thought we still had time—last night's moon wasn't even half full. Foxfire presses her chin to my shoulder, nosing me under the shelter of her chest and neck. I can feel her heart beating as fast as mine beneath her warm hair.

"Shh," I whisper again.

On the other side of the garden wall, a horse snorts. Low and calculating. Trying to take in certain smells. Does he smell her scent, apple and snow? Does he smell her wounded wing?

Clomp.

Clomp.

He's just outside the gate.

The gate!

It's open a crack—Bog must have nosed it open when he was going after that rabbit.

I duck out from the altar cloth and lunge for it, hoping

to get to it before the Black Horse can. My feet kick up snow as I push myself against it, trying to be quiet, and slide the willow branch through the metalwork to keep it closed. I force myself as still as the door itself, and close my eyes.

Has he heard me? Does he know?

He could fly over the gate, but he doesn't. Maybe he prefers to stalk us like foxes stalk their prey. The light through the cracks in the old gate mottles. There are footsteps. More of those investigating, low snorts. When I force my eyes open, I can just make out a shadow through the cracks. A tail. It is black and tangled into knots like the brambles that surround it.

There is a sudden kick at the gate. The wood buckles, and I shriek, and I push myself against it. Foxfire whinnies, peeking out from beneath the cloth. The gate buckles. He's going to get in!

"Go away!" I yell. "She isn't here! It's *me* you smell. It's the apple on *my* breath. It's the snow on *my* dress. It's *my* sickness you smell, not hers, so go away!"

And then a growl cuts through the air. Vicious barks come from the other side of the gate. Bog! But what is one old border collie against a winged monster?

And then a sudden *whoosh*, and a gust of air blows through the cracks in the gate strong enough to push me backward. A shadow rises high into the clouds, and the air shakes like thunder.

I throw the gate open.

"Bog!"

I'm afraid I'll see a little broken body torn apart just like my neighbor's cat did to that tiny little bird. But a white and black flash of movement comes from under a bench, and Bog trots through the gate, wagging his tail. I close the gate behind him, lock it with the willow stick, drop to my knees, and pull him close. His body is the same fur and bones and big wet nose that it always is.

"Thank you," I whisper into his big black eyes, and he licks my nose. Foxfire is peeking out from the cloth, ears pointed toward Bog and me. I go to her, pull the cloth back over her head, and rest my hand on her cheek. She doesn't shy away. She stretches out her left wing, flapping it until I come around to her side, and she can wrap her wing around me.

"And thank you, too," I say. "I promised to protect you, but you were the one who protected me. You warned me he was coming."

She shakes out her mane, almost like she is nodding.

I rest a hand on her withers. "You and me, we look out for each other. But I will take care of you a little extra, because I am your person, and you will always be my special horse."

I look back up at the sky.

Today, she is safe.

24

WHEN I RETURN TO the house, Dr. Turner's car is parked in the front.

It is strange—he usually parks neatly by the barn, but today the car is at an angle. When I climb in through the library window, I hear a commotion, which is also strange. Sunday afternoons are quiet. Sunday afternoons are plain bread and reading alone.

But a door slams, and someone starts coughing.

I am about to slip up the attic steps back to my room, but I get an odd feeling, like something isn't quite right. Someone is banging around downstairs in the kitchen. Sister Constance? But she leaves on Sunday afternoons to help the priest in Wick administer last rites to the townspeople who are dying of illness or old age. Then there are quick footsteps, and it's all I can do to jump into the linen closet and hide before both Sisters come striding down the hall.

"It started an hour ago," Sister Mary Grace says. "She's burning up."

I peek through the closet keyhole. Sister Constance is lugging a steaming copper pot with the handle wrapped in a towel. They open the door to Anna's room. The red ticket flutters in the gust and then falls down slowly, like a feather, and settles in the middle of the hallway.

I close my eyes.

I want to tell myself that I saw wrong. That it wasn't Anna's room, but Benny's, or anyone else's. But when I open my eyes, the door to Anna's room is still ajar.

I push my way out of the closet and walk toward the door with heavy steps. *Clomp, clomp,* like the clodding of a horse, except my boots make little noise on the hard floors. Dr. Turner's voice comes through the crack. He is giving Sister Constance orders. More coughing comes, but that can't be from Anna. Anna's coughs are quiet and ladylike, even when she is doubled over. This sounds like a soul being ripped apart.

Something crunches under my foot. The red ticket. The glue is still tacky, and it sticks to the sole of my boot and I start to panic, trying uselessly to kick it away.

"Emmaline." A voice whispers harshly at me from the

stairs. Benny sticks out his pinched face, shadows cast over his eyes. "Get back to your room."

"You don't tell me what to do," I say. He acts like Anna belongs to him as much as she does to me, just because she is kind to him, but she can't possibly matter to him the same way. Anna and I, we are like sisters.

Through the crack in Anna's door, I can see the back of Dr. Turner's white coat. Sister Mary Grace, dropping cloths in the steaming copper pot. More coughs, and I flinch.

I push open the door just a tiny, unnoticeable inch. Dr. Turner moves aside to gather his stethoscope, and I get a clear view. It *is* Anna. Her nightgown. Her light brown curls so like Marjorie's, though they are now soaked with sweat. Her face, though it is missing something. Her eyes are too dull.

All the sheets around her are soaked in blood.

"The morphine, Sister," Dr. Turner says. She passes him a needle, and he sticks it into a bare patch of Anna's skin, and then presses his stethoscope to her chest.

"It's too late. The lung has collapsed," he says.

Sister Mary Grace makes the sign of the cross.

I can see Anna's dresser mirror from here. There are winged horses in the reflection of her window. Their muzzles are pressed against the glass. They are watching. They are waiting.

I push the door open wider, and it catches Dr. Turner's

attention. He sees my reflection in the mirror and spins. The Sisters look up as well.

"Emmaline! You aren't to be here!" Sister Constance says.

I clutch the brass doorknob, hard. "What's going to happen to Anna?"

Sister Constance comes striding toward me. "To your room, young lady."

But as she reaches for me, I dart under her arm and sprint for the bed. Anna's room isn't big, even though it was once fit for a princess, and I'm able to grab the bedpost and jump on the mattress before they can stop me.

"Anna!" I cry.

I've never seen her face so pale. She reaches out an arm that is more bone than girl, and ruffles my tufts of hair.

"Emmaline."

Her voice is so weak that it breaks on the sound of my name. A sob comes out of my throat, and I crawl closer, until I can wrap my arms around her. "Anna, you'll get better. You'll be fine."

She is warm. Too warm. There is something inside her moving too fast, burning through everything she has.

"Em, I'm sorry I never saw your winged horses. I wanted to see them so badly. I kept looking at the mirrors. I did. But I never saw them. . . ."

She presses her cheek against mine.

She is fire. She is life. She is sickness.

Two hands grab me under the armpits. Sister Constance pulls me away with fingers like iron. "Emmaline, you can't be here!"

I tear at Sister Constance's hands. The black sleeves of her habit are rolled back, and my fingers rip her skin. "Let me go!"

But she doesn't. She pushes me through the open door. I try to scramble back inside, but Sister Mary Grace closes it and locks it. I claw at the wood. Pound on it. Tears are falling down my cheeks, and my middle finger is bleeding from where I clawed too hard.

"Anna!" I cry. "Anna, keep looking! They're there! They're right there! Do you see them?"

There is no answer. Only more coughing. Only Dr. Turner's low voice.

"Anna! Do you see them?"

Nothing.

I kick at the door. I look through the keyhole, but the key blocks my view. They must hear me pounding. How can they leave me out here? How can they tear me away from her, when she is my only friend? She is the only one who shares her colored pencils with me, and tells me stories of the floating gods, and whose stomach gurgles just like Mama's.

"Stop it!" Benny grabs my wrist. He is wearing a muddy-red sweater that matches his muddy-red hair and

I hate him, I hate him, I hate him. "You're acting like a child."

"They won't let me see her!"

"Dr. Turner needs to give her medicine without you crawling all over her and getting in the way. You're only thinking of yourself. You're a selfish little girl, and you have to grow up!"

My vision scatters into angry little dots. I twist out of Benny's hold and shove him, hard, so that he crashes to the floor.

"I hate you!"

I run down the hall. The mirrors lining the walls flash by. Winged horses stand in each one of them. Peering at me curiously as I run, their heads swiveling to follow my progress. I have never seen so many of them. They are everywhere.

And yet the hall is empty.

I run to the kitchen and shove open the back door, and I can't stop the coughs. They mix with sobs and I feel so shaky. Thomas is sitting on the stone steps with Bog at his side. They both jump up at the sound.

"Emmaline." He blinks like he wasn't expecting me. He swallows. "I heard Dr. Turner's car. Is it . . . is it Anna?" He wipes his hand on his trousers.

What do I say?

How can I tell him what is happening, when I don't even know myself?

I sink onto the highest step. I can't seem to draw in enough air.

And then a shadow passes over us. It ripples like water, but it is the shape of an airplane, only the wings move. They pull in. And extend again. A sound like thunder rolls through the air. Thomas's head pitches up, and he squints into the sky as a dark worry fills me.

"What is that?" he asks.

The shape is moving on the other side of the trees. Only a shadow, but I know what it is. Oh, I know. A creature that hunts by smell. A creature that I thought had left us alone, at least for today. A creature that is headed straight for the sundial garden.

25

"OH NO, HE'S BACK!"

Thomas calls after me as I race to the garden, but I don't respond. Winter chill nips through the layers of my clothing, and briars tear at my skin as I climb. Foxfire is pacing the wall, running in the tight space, back and forth. She too has seen the Black Horse's shadow, and I can tell we are thinking the same thing: It was only a trick, before. He never intended to leave us alone at all!

"Come on!" I yell to Foxfire. I rip out the stick holding the gate closed. My middle finger is bleeding all over everything, but I don't care. I turn to Foxfire. She can't fly, but she can still run.

"You have to leave! Run away as fast as you can!"

She's pacing wildly, rearing and pawing the air. She

doesn't know where to go. This is my world, not hers. I reach up and push her toward the open gate. Beyond are fields frosted and dead with winter. She is the same color as the frost. The Black Horse, with his poor vision, might not see her.

"Go!"

She tosses her head, throwing my hand away. She starts for the gate, but stops. Snorts. And then looks at me.

I know horses cannot talk. Even magic horses. But when I look into her eyes, I know what she is trying to say. Something eases deep in my chest. For a moment, as I find the strength to climb up the ivy, I don't feel the ache in my bones. From my height, I'm able to slide a hand over her shoulders. She doesn't buck. Doesn't snort a protest. I pull myself up by her withers, avoiding her hurt wing, and wrap my legs around either side of her.

I weave my fingers into her mane.

I have never ridden like this. No saddle. No reins. Wings on either side of my legs.

"Go!"

She tears through the gate. Her muscles are rippling beneath my legs, her quicksilver hooves pounding the frozen ground. I gasp with the thrill of it. The fields streak around us, and I lean into the bitter cold wind. If she is this fast running, what must she be like flying? I think she could outfly the Germans, if she wanted. She could certainly outfly a Black Horse.

There is only the wind and Foxfire and me. We are one.

I clutch her mane harder and look over my shoulder. We are jostling, jostling, jostling, and the hospital disappears from view as we plunge down Briar Hill into empty fields. I've never seen the hospital from a distance. It looks so grand. Lights are shining in all of the windows. The two oaks in the front lawn rise like sentries.

A dark shadow ripples beside us, matching us in time.

"Faster, faster!"

And she does. She goes faster. She goes faster than I thought a horse could go. Some other part of me takes over. Presses my legs closer to her. Leans in. The wind cuts right through me, but I don't feel it. I don't hear Anna coughing. I don't feel Benny's thin hand on my wrist. There is only the wind and Foxfire and me. We are one.

"Don't stop!"

Tears are coming faster down my face. The wind freezes them before they can fall. I hug my arms around Foxfire's neck and want never to let her go. We reach the end of the field, and Foxfire leans hard to the left, circling the line of willows that skirt the stream. She slows, just a little. It isn't until she has circled the field three times that I realize I haven't seen the black shadow in some time.

She continues to slow until she switches to a trot that has me bouncing on the hard bones of her back. The gray sky is bare now. A few clouds, but no Black Horse.

We have escaped him—really escaped him—for one more day.

Foxfire slows to a walk, and I press my left leg into her side. She is a wild horse, so she does not know the signals, but she seems to understand. She circles around and heads back to the open garden gate.

We return to the fountain and the tarnished sundial. I slide off her back, feet catching on the fountain's rim, and then hop off onto the ground.

She bows her head to me, and I press my hands to the sides of her face. I touch my forehead to the swirl of her horse-hair that is the shape of a spark, right between her eyes.

"I won't let him get you. I made a promise, and I'll keep it."

Foxfire tosses her head again. She is breathing hard, and turns to take a long drink from the fountain.

Tomorrow I will find the last colors.

I will find something blue.

I will find something orange.

I will find something to keep the Black Horse far, far away from this protected place.

I trudge back to the hospital with feet that feel numb but a heart that feels alive.

All the lights are on in the windows. Thomas isn't sitting on the steps anymore. There is no sign of Bog. When I push open the kitchen door, no one is sitting at the table, though the clock says it's past suppertime.

I hold my hands over the woodstove until I can feel

them again, and take down one of the big towels from the linen closet and wrap myself in it. I've started shivering, now that feeling is coming back into my body. Deep shivering that cuts to the bone. My legs are so weak that walking is getting hard. Each step up the stairs burns. I wipe my dripping nose.

The hallway is lined with children, all sitting quietly. They seem like they have been there for some time. Jack looks up. He isn't crying. Benny looks up too. He is.

The door to Anna's room opens, and Sister Mary Grace stands in the doorway. Her shoulders are stooped—it doesn't look right on a woman of her young age. The sleeves of her habit are pushed back as she wipes her hands with a towel.

Her eyes are red.

"Oh, Emmaline," she says softly when she sees me.

And I know. I *know.* She doesn't have to say it. I don't want her to. I want to exist in this moment alone. The moment when I have saved Foxfire, even if just for one day, and this moment when Anna is still alive and tomorrow I will draw her a picture and she will tell me a story about the floating gods on the ceiling.

"Emmaline, I'm sorry."

The horses are gone from the mirrors. I do not know where they go, when they leave.

She pushes the door open farther as she comes out

into the hall, and I see Thomas, sitting on a chair next to Anna's bed.

He looks at me.

And then, he sees something in the mirror across the hall and turns. I follow his gaze. There is one winged horse. One winged horse that we both see. It bows its beautiful brown head, and stretches its brown wings.

Deep in my chest, the stillwaters are rising.

"Anna is gone," Sister Mary Grace says.

There is a comfort in sheep.

26

THERE IS A COMFORT IN SHEEP.

It isn't just that they are soft and warm (though sometimes a bit dirty). It isn't their bleating, or the way the little lambs climb all over each other. It is not their sheep-smell, which the other children dislike but I don't mind. It isn't their pink tongues. It is the way you can say not a single word, but not feel alone.

The barn door opens.

Thomas comes in, wiping his nose against the cold, and takes the shovel from its hook on the wall. The sheep bleat for food, and he sees me sitting in their midst. He stops.

"Did you fall asleep here?"

I nod.

"A priest has come, and Anna's family. You'll miss the funeral."

In my hands, I hold a small box wrapped in newspaper and tied with a bit of twine that Sister Mary Grace gave me. "I know."

He doesn't say any more. Thomas's quiet ways used to scare me, but now, I am thankful for them. I'm tired of Sister Constance and Sister Mary Grace and Dr. Turner and the other children talking. I just want to be with sheep. Alone, but not lonely.

Something ugly stirs in my chest, and I cough into the straw and wipe my mouth. My face feels warm. Too warm. Burning.

"The altar cloth . . . ," he starts, a bit hesitantly. "I thought you might want to know that Sister Constance decided to use the black one in the chapel, to mourn Anna. They'll leave it up for at least another week. Longer, maybe." He bends down to right Bog's ear, which is always flopping over.

And I can tell, in the way that he doesn't quite meet my eyes, that he knows that I stole the purple Advent cloth. He must have seen me sneaking across the grounds with it stuffed in my coat. And now he is telling me that I won't be caught. At least, not today.

Anna has helped me again. I am glad for Foxfire's sake, but I would rather be caught and punished by Sister Constance every day for a year and have Anna back.

I nod.

Thomas touches his cap and leaves.

I know that Anna's service is unfolding in the chapel. In the six months I have been here, one other child has died, a boy who came in the middle of the night, so ill that he was gone by the next morning. His service was small and short, and I know Anna's will be the same. Sister Constance is nothing if not practical. There are bills to be paid. Living children to be fed. A leaking faucet that needs repair.

A sheep lets out a long sheep-sigh, and rests its chin on my leg. I scratch its bony head, and its eyes half close. I rub my other thumb over the package's twine, tied in such a prim little bow.

Sister Mary Grace came all the way up to my attic last night after supper. She brought me a dusty old bar of chocolate on a tray—I don't know where she'd had it hidden away—and this package, too.

"Christmas isn't for a few days," she said. "But I want you to have an early present. Well, Anna wanted you to have it. Sometimes people die when they get too sick, and there is nothing we can do but let them return to the Lord."

In the barn, I run my thumb along the corners of the package, its paper worn from me handling it all morning, afraid to open it. I know this shape. I know this size. I know exactly what I will find when I pull loose that twine and strip off the paper.

The bell tolls outside. Thomas will come back soon

with the shovel, clods of dirt from the southern slope on his boots.

I open the brown paper and brown twine. Beneath it lie all the colors of the rainbow. I open the top flap of the colored pencil box and breathe in the smell of wood and paint.

The little sheep with its chin on my leg starts to snore. I curl up next to it, hugging Anna's box of colored pencils.

27

I DON'T SEE FOXFIRE for days. I can't. I am so sad about Anna that my limbs don't want to move. I am so sad and angry with God that I just want to hide and cry. Sister Mary Grace frowns when she takes my temperature, and takes pity on me and lets me skip classes to draw quietly in my bedroom instead. But then a swollen half-moon comes and casts a dangerous glow over the world beyond my attic window.

And I know: I must be strong for Foxfire, even now. The Horse Lord is depending on me.

I wait until Sister Constance is in her office and the other children are in the classroom working on letters home to their families, and sneak out through the library window. I won't be missed. They think I'm in the attic.

My legs are so weak that the walk to the sundial garden

feels longer than ever before. The climb over the wall feels like a mountain. But when I drop down, Foxfire is there.

She looks up at me.

And *oh*, how I have missed her.

I had forgotten her apple smell. I had forgotten her silken hair. I had forgotten how alive I felt with her soft dark eyes on me, the small nod of her head that says she missed me, just as I missed her.

And yet, strangely, there is no letter from the Horse Lord. Days have passed. I expected an entire stack of letters, especially as the full moon is only a week away, but there is nothing.

An uneasy feeling makes my hand tremble, but I manage to write a new note on a scrap of paper I brought with me, and tuck it under the sundial:

Dear Horse Lord,

Why haven't you written? Are you all right? I do not know if you know this, but the Black Horse tried to attack. He is so wicked, so mean, that I truly hate him! But Foxfire is safe, and I am surrounding her with every colorful object I can find, though I do not know if it will be enough. Sometimes horses die when they get too sick. I do not want her to die. Please tell me what to do.

Truly,
Emmaline May

And then, it's Christmas Eve.

And then, it's Christmas Eve. I don't know how Christmas can arrive without Anna, but it does, and Sister Mary Grace tells me I must not keep to myself anymore.

Our families are not allowed to visit, but Mr. Mason from the farm next door comes in the afternoon, when the shadows are long, with a Christmas tree. He pulls it in his donkey cart and stands outside, talking to the Sisters, who rub their bare hands in the cold. We all watch with our faces pressed against the glass.

"We've never had a tree before," Peter says. He and Jack have been here the longest now, and have seen two Christmases at the hospital. "Sister Constance says Christmas is about Christ's birth, not Saint Nicholas."

"The Americans sent presents last year," Jack says wistfully, nose pressed to the glass. "Enough to fill the whole chapel, but the Sisters only let us keep one each. I got my steam engine train. And now it's gone missing." He is silent, and I turn away, and hope my cheeks are not burning too red.

After a few tense moments of argument outside, when the donkey starts hee-hawing from the cold, Sister Constance throws up her hands. The farmer grins, and lifts the tree to his shoulder.

The other children cheer.

I watch the snow falling, standing apart from them all. It doesn't feel right. Not without Anna. And now without the Horse Lord, too.

Then a tree is coming straight through the front door and into the library, filling the room with forest smells, and leaving a trail of sap and needles in its wake. "Benny, go find Thomas," Sister Mary Grace says, "and have him fetch a bucket and some screws."

Benny darts off down the hall.

"Emmaline, get a pot of water."

I rub at my eyes, feeling too exhausted even to move. But then my eye catches on a flash of color. It's a crumpled old handkerchief Mr. Mason is using to wipe the sap off his hands. He starts to stuff it back in his pocket but frowns at the sap, and tosses the worn hankie into our scrap bin instead, and my heart starts to *thump, thump, thump* in a way it hasn't since Anna died. The handkerchief is a little frayed, but the color is unmistakable. *868*-LAPIS BLUE.

Sister Mary Grace is looking at me curiously, as though she is tempted to take my temperature again.

I force myself to stand on shaky legs. "Yes, Sister. I'll get the water." I make my way to the kitchen, winded after just a few steps, where I take down a copper pot and set it in the sink. As I wait for it to fill, I look at my reflection in the pot's side: Sunken eyes. Pale skin. There are two winged horses standing behind me, their wings outstretched, almost as though to shelter me from rain, though there is no rain indoors.

I carry the pot back to the library and stand close to the farmer. He and Thomas act like they're building a war machine, with all the engineering that goes into getting that tree to stand up straight in the bucket. I lean in, pretending to watch, and very quietly reach down and draw the handkerchief out of the scrap paper bin. I cough as I stuff it into my boot.

He won't miss it, surely. To him, it is just an old, worn-out scrap he threw away. To me—to Foxfire—it is hope.

They finish, though the tree still slopes a little at the top. Mr. Mason tells us we must water it every day. He tells us we must be very careful, when we tie candles to the branches, that it not catch fire.

"And best set out cookies for Saint Nick," he says with a wink.

Sister Constance's mouth goes grim.

We watch through the windows as he lights his cart's lantern, and leads the poor frozen donkey back home.

"Let's make decorations!" Kitty squeaks. "We can make a paste out of lye. It'll look just like snow on the tree."

The children jump up. They start tearing through the scraps of fabric and ribbon that Sister Mary Grace brings out in her sewing kit. Others drag down dusty boxes from the attic, where Arthur finds shiny red metal Christmas balls that he gazes at with delight. Two of the three little mice run outside to gather pinecones, and Sister Constance doesn't even say anything about the no-going-beyond-the-kitchen-terrace rule.

I glance out the open door, wondering when I can slip away to the garden to string up the handkerchief. Thomas, at some point, must have slipped away himself. I wonder if he is back in the barn, with Bog and the sheep. I wonder if he likes to be alone but not lonely too.

Susan holds up a string of white paper chains. "It's so plain." She suddenly spins on me. "Fetch the colored pencils Anna gave you! We can color the links green and red!"

The other children look up at me, their sticky fingers covered in paste.

Dread darkens me like a shadow. The pencils? *Anna's* pencils? But she gave them to *me*.

I shake my head.

Benny huffs and looks at Sister Constance. "Tell her she must share!"

"Anna gave them to her," Sister Constance says. "She can do what she wishes with them. If she chooses the path of generosity, as Anna so often did, then she will bring out the colored pencils. If she chooses to be selfish, well, then that is her choice."

"But she's being a baby!" Benny folds his arms, glaring. There is a wooden cross of Christ strung up behind him. If Jesus's hands weren't nailed to the cross, I think he'd be folding them at me too.

I fold my arms and glare right back.

If they want color—real color—then they are looking in the wrong places.

Benny glowers at me, then scoops up a handful of the snow paste on impulse.

"We *all* miss her!"

He throws the paste at my face.

It fills my mouth with the sudsy taste of lye. I sputter and cough, and Sister Constance grabs Benny by the ear.

"That wasn't called for," she admonishes.

"She's a selfish little monster," Benny spits out, while his ear is rapidly turning red. "She can't just ... She isn't the only one ..."

He disappears as Sister Constance drags him away, muttering something about staying in his room until the isolation makes his brain work properly.

I glance in the window's reflection. The paste has turned my skin into a clumpy mess.

The other children are fighting the urge to snicker.

A monster.

The others won't say it aloud, not with Sister Mary Grace's watchful gaze right there, but I know they are thinking it.

Thomas is a monster because he is missing something.

I am a monster because I have too much of something. Too much hurt. Too much rage.

I do not care.

Only monsters, it seems, know that there are worlds and worlds and worlds, and ours is only one.

28

FOR DAYS, I CANNOT sneak out of the house. The Sisters stay up late during the holidays, writing cards to the village boys at war, in the library beside the window with the broken lock. I wait in the dark of the stairs, alone, rubbing my tired eyes, until at last they leave and I can dart outside to knot the farmer's blue handkerchief into the ivy wall. There is still no letter from the Horse Lord, only my last one soggy and stained, and it leaves me feeling sick, as though I've eaten spoiled ham.

Back in my attic room, I cannot sleep.

The wind is knocking at the window. *Thump. Thump.* It is the same sound as horses kicking at a stall to be set free. I am sweating, even though the wind slipping through the cracks is frigid. No matter how much I ball up the blankets, the cold still gets in. I start to call to Papa to put more coal on the fire, but then I remember.

Papa isn't here.

The day he left for the war, Mama and Marjorie and I dressed in our Sunday clothes. Marjorie combed my hair back into a ribbon, and she held my hand while we stood on the curb, watching the men parade down Waverley Street toward Castle Green, eating plump cherries Mama had brought, cheering, pointing out the men we knew from church and school, snickering at how serious the bakery delivery boys looked in uniform.

And Papa. Papa, with his wide shoulders strong as a workhorse, with his chocolate-colored hair, and that moment—a moment anyone else would have missed— when he saw us cheering for him and had to hold back a proud smile. It wasn't until that night at supper, when I saw his empty chair at the head of the table, that the echo of the trumpets in my ears started to feel hollow.

I stare at the attic rafters. There are no spiderwebs. There are no swirls of dust. Sister Mary Grace can do one true thing to fight the stillwaters, and that is keep everything very clean, and so that is what she does.

I start coughing and double over, and something falls off my quilt and rolls across the floor. I collapse back on my pillow, feeling shaky and both cold and hot at the same time, and it is then that I recognize that rolling sound of the fallen object.

A pencil.

I strike a match and light a candle, then lean over to peer at the floor.

868-LAPIS BLUE.

The pencil is on the floor. In two separate pieces.

Broken!

Have I just broken it?

I scramble toward it so fast that I pitch clear out of bed and land on the hard floor. I pick up the two pieces. The end is broken off and dulled, the body snapped clear in two, and my heart pounds as I think of ways to fix it. *Stick it back together. Glue the pieces.* There must be a way. . . .

The candle flickers, and another burst of color under the bed catches my eye. *845*-CARMINE RED. Except it is only a tiny piece. The point of the pencil. With dread, I lift the quilt.

I almost cannot tell you what happens next.

It is too, too terrible.

The pencils. All of them. *849*-TANGERINE ORANGE and *876*-HELIOTROPE PURPLE and *867*-SEA TURQUOISE. Broken. Shattered. They've been stomped on and splintered and stamped out. The candlelight flickers over them, illuminating the crime scene. And one of my drawings, crumpled. I pull it out with shaking fingers.

The horse's wings have been crossed out with black pencil, hard enough to tear the paper.

TIME TO GROW UP, someone has written.

Someone.

Oh, I know who.

I want to race downstairs and throw myself on his bed and strangle his gangly neck while he sleeps. I want to rip his precious comic book to shreds. I want to stomp on *him*, splinter *him*, break *him* into pieces.

Thump, thump.

I gasp and pitch my head up. What's that? The Black Horse—he's back. His hooves stomp on the roof and suddenly it is *him* I want to break. He's the cause of everything that is wrong, I know it.

The winged horses in the mirrors watch me as I sneak down the hall, slip on my coat and boots, and climb out the library window. Overhead, the moon is so very nearly full, and I hate it too. I drag my bare fingers through the snow, pressing it into balls, and hurl them at the roof as hard as I can.

"Get away!" I yell.

I throw another snowball. And another. But my arm is weak and they only hit the first-floor windows. It is too dark to see if the Black Horse is up there, or if it is just shadows. But it doesn't matter. I know he is there.

He is always there.

A light comes on in one of the windows, and I drop my snowball. I drag myself toward the garden wall, forcing my weak limbs to climb up and over before anyone can look outside and see me. I hurry, winded, through the maze of gardens. Through the rose garden with the rotting trellises, around the broken fountains, past the overgrown azalea garden, until I reach the sundial garden. Foxfire swings her head at me, ears swiveling forward in anticipation of an apple.

I stomp straight up to her.

"The Horse Lord never should have sent you here!" I yell, fighting the tightness in my lungs. "This isn't a protected place. Our world is no safer than yours. If the Black Horse can find you there, he can find you here. It's just a matter of time! Bad things happen here, don't you see? Anna is gone. My pencils are destroyed. And the Horse Lord won't even write. He's abandoned us both. There's no point in fighting anymore, do you hear me? There's no point!"

And it's true. He hasn't written. He's forgotten about us. Anna died and left me. The Horse Lord left me too.

But I stop.

Wait.

There is a fresh note tucked into the sundial. The same creamy white paper. Tied in the same red ribbon.

With shaking hands, I pull it free.

Dear Emmaline May,

You must forgive me for the brief lapse in letters. I was struck with a minor illness that leaves a tremor in my hand; no doubt you will notice that my script is altered.

You asked how long the winged horses live. All I can say is that they live much longer than I. Perhaps a hundred years. Perhaps they never die at all. I quite believe that myself, and it is a comfort, don't you think? That there is a place where no one ever grows old? You see, our worlds are more connected than you believe. Sometimes, when a special person in your world dies before his or her time, that person merely crosses over and becomes one of my horses, roaming the heavens on feathered wings.

Ride true,
The Horse Lord

I read the note again. The cold makes my nose run. I think of the broken colored pencils that Anna kept perfectly sharpened. I think of Anna's empty bed. The Sisters haven't changed anything about it but the sheets, though I heard Benny saying they were going to move out her big bed and replace it with three cots, for three new children who will come soon.

I think back to that time I hid behind the woodpile and watched Thomas bury the chicken that the foxes had killed. He touched its feathers before covering them with dirt. I wonder if he did the same when he helped bury Anna.

If he presses his fingers against the pine boxes stacked in the barn that he built to bury those of us who die, and what he feels against his fingertips.

I wipe my nose.

"I have to go," I say to Foxfire. "I'm sorry, but it's important. Don't worry, I'll keep protecting you. I'll find something orange before the full moon, I promise."

Foxfire nuzzles my neck with her nose. I press my forehead to her spark blaze.

We understand each other, she and I.

And then I turn back to the wall, and climb.

29

I RUN THROUGH THE FROSTED FIELDS until I reach Thomas's cottage next to the barn. Wisps of smoke come from the chimney.

Knock, knock.

Bog stirs first, growling low, but Thomas gives a *ssss*, and Bog is silent. There are footsteps. Then the door swings open.

Thomas's head drops down, as though he was expecting someone taller. "Emmaline?" His empty sleeve is not carefully pinned now. It hangs loose and hollow as he rubs his sleepy eyes with his hand. "What's wrong?" He looks around to see if I am alone. "You can't keep sneaking out so late. It's getting colder and you're..." He pauses as I double over to cough. "You don't want to get any worse," he finishes.

"I need to show you something," I cough out. "It's important."

He rubs the sleep from his eyes once more, and glances at the hospital as if he has half a mind to walk me back there and turn me in to Sister Constance. But he stifles a yawn, and opens the door wider.

I hesitate.

I have never been in Thomas's cottage. None of us has. Benny says it is the place that he takes his victims to cage them until the witches eat them, but I see no children in cages. I see no swords or knives. I see only a rope bed with a straw mattress, like mine but bigger, and a woodstove with a coffeepot on top, and a few shirts hung in the rafters to dry.

There *is* a gnawed bone on the floor—but I think it belongs to Bog.

Thomas closes the door behind me to keep the heat in. He rubs his chin. "What is so important in the middle of the night?"

The heat from the woodstove makes my armpits damp. I fumble for the Horse Lord's letter, starting to feel silly. Maybe this could have waited until the morning. Maybe it is childish to be here.

But no. Some things cannot wait.

I hand him the letter. "Read it."

But he doesn't take it.

"Well, go ahead."

He clears his throat. He shakes his head, keeping his eyes on the woodstove. "Groundskeepers only read the weather."

I'm a bit flustered—perhaps he cannot read and is embarrassed—and I take back the letter and read aloud the part about the special people who die before their time. When I'm finished, I look at him expectantly.

His brow is knit together like he doesn't understand.

"That's what I came to tell you," I explain. "That certain special people who die before their time become winged horses. Your father, I mean. He was a great man who died before his time." I tuck the letter back into my pocket. "Death isn't the end for him. The Horse Lord says so."

Thomas looks at the woodstove. Then he presses his thumb and forefinger against the bridge of his nose, and takes a deep breath. He reaches down and rests his hand on my head. His palm is broad. It's clear he is a man of the land, of the soil, but that doesn't mean he isn't a man of the heart, too.

"If the Horse Lord said it," he says, "then it must be true."

"And for Anna, too."

He nods. "For Anna, too."

"And for me, if I die from the stillwaters."

His hand, patting my short hair, stops. Bog looks up from gnawing on the bone, and cocks his head. Thomas takes a deep breath. The Sisters get upset whenever we talk like this. Asking about what happens if we die. They say it is our duty to think about life, not death, and to eat our bread and leave such matters to God. Dr. Turner gets upset too. He says many children survive the stillwaters. He tells us we could very well go on to live long lives, and become wives and mothers and husbands and doctors.

Thomas gives a soft sort of smile. "If that happens," he says, "then you'll fly the fastest of all the horses, I know it."

30

THE NEXT DAY, the snow turns to stinging little pellets. Sister Constance's strained voice carries from the classroom; she is teaching the little ones how to do basic sums. In the residence hall, all the older children's doors are halfway open as they study from dog-eared textbooks with small print and no pictures.

I make for the attic stairs. Maybe there is a trunk I missed in one of the storerooms. Some long-forgotten package, filled with dusty paper that I'll lift with care, to find a vase gleaming the color of tangerine orange. There used to be orange all over the world, I remember. At Christmas, oranges in our stockings. The oak tree's leaves in autumn. Marigolds in spring.

But it is not spring.

It is not autumn.

It is winter, and there are no tangerines this year, not even with ration booklets. And without the color orange, the spectral shield is not complete. It is not strong enough to keep the Black Horse away.

I turn the corner, and stop.

The weight of eyes is on my back. I spin.

The hall is empty.

The only sound is snoring coming from Rodger's bedroom. But when I turn back toward the attic stairs, the sensation returns, and I spin around again, and then again, in a full circle. The hair on the back of my neck tingles and—and is that the smell of apples? Movement in the hall mirror catches my eye. One of the winged horses steps into view in the gilded frame. He has a gray snip on his nose. He presses his muzzle against his side of the glass so that it fogs with each breath from his nostrils.

He is looking right at me.

"Um ... hello." I take a slow step closer. I reach up toward the mirror, but he pulls away, and my first two fingers brush only cold glass.

He tosses his head, and then snorts once, twice, and prances away. The mirror is once again just my own plain face looking back, short tufts of hair and green eyes and two sticky fingerprints.

But then—*there*. Movement from the next mirror down the hall, back the way I've just come. The same winged horse with the gray snip on his nose is there now, shaking his head so the ropes of his mane fall in his eyes. I reach for him, but he tosses his head again and disappears. Just like the bakery horses used to do with my sister, Marjorie. Letting her come close, close, close . . . and then prancing away. It was a game they played.

I rest my hands on my hips.

"I don't have time for games."

But he tosses his head again and prances off. In another moment he appears in the next mirror down the hall. He taps his nose against the glass. When I don't come closer, he taps it again, more insistently this time, and rubs so hard against the glass that I'm afraid it will break.

"You aren't playing a game, are you?" I whisper. "You're trying to tell me something."

He disappears out of that mirror as well, and I can almost feel the brush of his wings in the air as he passes down the same hall, only in a different world. And then he's at the last mirror. Almost as though he is beckoning me to follow. When I reach the mirror, he doesn't leave this time. He tosses his head. Steam frosts his side of the mirror.

He nudges the glass. Again and again, as if trying to nuzzle me, though his black eyes are on something behind me. I turn around. Benny's room is across the hall. The door is open halfway. There is no sign of Benny or the other boys. Probably sneaked off to smoke another cigarette.

"What do you see?" I whisper.

And then my eyes fall on Benny's bed, and my heart forgets to beat, just once, just for a second. Right there on the gray wool blanket is Benny's precious Popeye comic book. The cover is an explosion of bright orange ink.

849-TANGERINE ORANGE.

I tiptoe in for a closer look. Yes. This is exactly what I have been looking for! I pick it up and flip open the cover, hardly daring to believe my good luck, and find a note written in the margins of the first page.

Benny,

Found this at Blakeway Books—a Popeye we haven't read yet!

Love,
Dad

I quickly drop the comic book on the bed and take a few steps backward. Benny's father gave this to him. Benny has a father off fighting somewhere, just like I do. My stomach is doing flip-flops. This is why he reads and re-reads this comic so much, even though comic books are childish things. It is something to hold on to, something from before. And suddenly I miss my papa, my mama, and Marjorie, and the smell of apple pie on cold winter mornings.

I spin toward the mirror. "I don't know if I can take this. It matters to him."

But the horse is gone. Only my face looks back. Teeth a little uneven. Nose too red.

And then another face appears behind me, and I freeze. Unfortunately, this face is on *my* side of the mirror.

"What do you think you're doing?" Benny snaps. He folds his arms, awaiting my answer.

I glance at the comic book from the corner of my eye, thankful that I put it back exactly where he left it. "None of your business."

His expression darkens. "You're supposed to be up in your room, not down here, snooping through ..." He glances at his bed, and sees the book. "What are you up to, you little thief?"

"I'm not a thief!"

But my cheeks flame with the lie as I think of Jack's toy train, and the princess's belongings in the attic, and Dr. Turner's medicine bottle.

Benny reaches suddenly for my pocket and pulls out the Horse Lord's latest letter. I gasp and snatch for it, but he holds it over my head.

"What's this, then?"

"It's addressed to me!"

His forehead wrinkles in confusion. "Who would write *you* a letter?" He unrolls it, reading it quickly.

"Give it back!"

But he holds me off with one bony hand while he finishes reading. Then he crumples it in his fist, turning to me with a sneer, and the rawboned hound is back. "The Horse Lord?" And then he starts laughing. I slap and claw at him, but he doesn't seem to feel it. He laughs so hard he has to wipe a tear out of his eye. "Who wrote this? Dr. Turner?"

"The Horse Lord is real! We've been writing to each other for weeks. I told you about the winged horses in the mirrors and in the garden. You didn't believe me, but it's true."

His eyes waver as though he's almost afraid what I'm saying is true and that *he's* going to look like the fool for teasing me. But then he blinks. "Someone is playing a joke on you, Emmaline."

"No."

"It's probably Dr. Turner. Only he could get paper this nice. But then again, Sister Mary Grace does have all that ribbon...."

"Ask Thomas," I snap. "He's seen the winged horses too."

Benny's face lights up. "Thomas! Of course. You dolt, Thomas is the one writing these letters. Only it isn't a joke at all. It's a trap." His eyes go wide, as he holds the letter high out of my reach. I strain on tiptoes for it, and we spin around and around as he drops his voice. "Didn't you listen to the stories? He's trying to lure you into his cottage so he can make you into shepherd's pie!"

"That isn't true!" I'm screaming now, and the other children peek at us through the cracks in their doors. "Thomas can't even write!"

"There is no Horse Lord. There are no winged horses. They're all in your head."

The angry words on my lips die. I stop spinning, legs weak, and collapse against the wall. A door squeaks as one of the children accidentally bumps it too hard. Benny glances up and sees our audience. For a second, he doesn't seem to know what to do. A dozen hallway mirrors reflect his raised hand in the air, the Horse Lord's letter crumpled in it, the red ribbon dangling.

He lets the letter fall and stomps on it with his shoe.

"Get to your room," Benny commands. "And the rest of you, stay away from Thomas. I warned you."

He glares at me with that hound-face of his, and then struts into his room and flops on his bed. He snatches up the Popeye comic book, flipping through the pages deliberately.

So orange.

As orange as his hair. As orange as fire.

They are all in your head.

Some of the children snicker. I hear giggling about flying horses and make-believe princes. The mirrors are all empty now. But the horses were there. The one with the gray snip on his nose, who led me to Benny's comic book. He was real. And the letter . . . *No. It can't be.*

I fall to my knees and try to smooth the letter out the best I can, but the writing is smudged from Benny's shoe. I feel the urge to cry. The red ribbon is torn. I eye it sidelong, wiping away the start of tears. *Is* it like the spools in Sister Mary Grace's sewing kit? And the paper ... *is* it like Dr. Turner's prescription forms? But no, his forms are perforated. These have crisp edges.

Benny is wrong. Benny doesn't know the first thing about winged horses.

I glance toward his open door. He flips another page and snickers at Popeye.

I almost want the Black Horse to come. I almost want to summon him myself so he will take Benny and all the children who are laughing. I want the Black Horse to tear through the hospital roof with midnight hooves and thorn-tangled tail and thunder down the hallways loud enough to break every mirror and catch Benny under his hooves until all that is left of Benny is as crumpled and broken as this letter.

But the Black Horse doesn't want Benny.

I pick up the letter. I am going to get that comic book.

31

I BIDE MY TIME. Benny has been trailing me, following my every move. He never has his comic book with him, so he must have hidden it, just as I have hidden the broken colored pencils in the secret drawer of Anna's desk. But at last he gets lazy. He gets bored. He gets careless. And while the children are gathered in Sister Constance's office listening to a broadcast by Winston Churchill on the radio, I make my move.

There is a winged horse in the residence hall mirror behind me, one I've never seen, with pretty blue eyes, swatting her tail at flies in the mirror-hallway. She watches me curiously as I tiptoe closer to the very last door on the right of the residence hall.

Benny's door.

I ease it open and close it behind me. Only once I'm in the room do I breathe out.

There are three beds, but I know which one is his. Even if I didn't, the smell of onions would give it away. I tiptoe over and lift his pillow: no comic book. I slide open his bedside table: nothing but a bag of old nuts and letters from home. I drop down to look under the bed: nothing.

I sit on the bed, thinking. I have to find it.

If I were a nasty, hound-faced boy, where would I hide my comic book?

My eyes fall to the big Bible on his desk, and I remember him reading Popeye last Sunday instead of the Bible. I flip it open, and a few pages in, Popeye looks back at me. My eyes go wide. What would God think of *that*?

I grab the comic book and stuff it down my shirt just as footsteps sound in the hallway. Through the cracked door, I watch the winged horse in the mirror pace back and forth, blue eyes wide, as though to warn me. I drop down and crawl under Benny's bed just as the footsteps stop at the bedroom door. Black boots. Narrow width. Sister Mary Grace's. The urge to cough rises, and I clamp a hand over my mouth. She stands still for a moment, and then closes the door.

I wait.

The floor under his bed is sticky, and there's a fallen

nut or two. I cannot stay here long. The radio broadcast will end soon, and he will return. I cough into my hand as quietly as I can.

I crawl out slowly, blood pounding in my ears, and twist the doorknob. Outside, the hall is quiet. The winged horse with the blue eyes has her back to me, as though she is asleep. I take a deep breath, and then tiptoe down the hall on sock feet and dart into Anna's bedroom. They haven't taken out her big bed and heavy furniture yet. I press the hidden lever on the underside of the desk that releases the secret drawer. It pops open, and suddenly the room is filled with Anna again. Dried lavender. Her naturalist books. A single fine black-ink pen and the broken pencils I placed there for safekeeping. I shove the comic book in and close the drawer, and then dash out. I veer at the hall corner and go flying by, ducking beneath the door of Sister Constance's office and onto the attic stairs just as the broadcast ends and the children emerge into the hall.

I stop to catch my breath at the top of the stairs, in the shadows where no one looks.

In the dark, I smile.

32

"WHERE IS IT?"

Benny's shouts carry all the way to the top of the attic stairs. I draw in a sharp breath, but that triggers the coughing again. I can barely muffle it against my sleeve.

Outside the attic window, the late afternoon sun sinks farther. Soon the moon will rise. Nearly a *full* moon. I only have one day to spare, as tomorrow the moon will be completely round and bright. I need to sneak out to the sundial garden. I need to set the comic book in its place on the wall of ivy. I need to complete the spectral shield to protect Foxfire. All eight rainbow colors just like in the manufacturer's description. A complete set.

And yet.

As soon as I stand up from the stairs, my vision goes

black, and I immediately sit down again. My lungs. The beast that waits there, deep beneath the stillwaters, is clawing at my throat.

I throw a hand over my mouth. Not now. Please. Not tonight.

I try to think soothing thoughts: Water flowing down my throat. Warm melted chocolate. Fresh milk straight from the pail. But the tickle won't be ignored. It grows into a briary rose that someone is scratching up and down the insides of my throat.

"NO!" Benny yells. "Someone took it!"

There are frantic footsteps and more shouting from beyond the attic door. Benny saw me sneaking around in his room. Benny has sharp eyes like a hunting dog. He will know it was me.

But he can search my room all he wants—he won't find it.

I take one long look outside. Is Foxfire waiting for me? Is the Black Horse blinking, clearing his vision, waiting for the light of tomorrow's full moon so he can attack again? But my limbs are shaking and my vision is going wavy and it's all I can do to crawl to my attic room. One inch at a time, each step its own small battle, and I think of the men in the rubble, lungs choked with dust from German bombs, crawling and crawling to safety. At last, I reach my bedroom. I kick the door shut and lean against it, breathing hard. The stillwaters beast is not going to calm down this time. It came for Anna and now Anna is gone and it wants more lungs to thrash around in, other throats to claw and shred.

I pull myself onto the rope mattress and collapse on the quilt. The cough comes freely now. I let it. It shreds the inside of my throat, forcing its way out. I feel like someone is wringing me out. No water left. No life left. I taste the bitter bite of blood. Beyond the doors, there come angry footsteps stomping up the stairs.

They stop outside of my door.

KNOCK, KNOCK.

Benny's voice. "I know it was you, you thief!"

The door opens a few inches. Benny's angry face haunts the crack, his sharp eyes hunting around the room, his spindly nose sniffing. Then he sees me and his eyes go wide. "Emmaline? Are you . . ." He stumbles back. "Sister Constance, come quick! There's blood everywhere!"

His footsteps going down the stairs are even faster.

I smile. It is the last thing I remember, before my head lolls back. I smile, and think of the rainbow that Marjorie and I saw that day in the rain. I was afraid it would be the last one I'd ever see.

But soon. Soon. I will finish my own.

33

MARJORIE IS SITTING ON the edge of my bed, wearing her yellow raincoat, reading Benny's comic book. She smells like fresh apple pie and cinnamon, and oh, I have missed that smell. I have missed *her*. My sister. I try to sit up, but my head is so heavy that I crash right back down against the pillows. The attic feels too warm. I want to throw off the covers, but Marjorie is sitting on them firmly.

"That comic . . ." My voice doesn't sound like my own. The stillwaters beast has shredded my throat. "Put it back. Keep it hidden. . . ."

She flips a page and smiles at a drawing of Popeye riding a camel. "You worry too much, Em. You always worried too much." She flips another page. My head feels like only half of it is there, but where would the other half be?

And why is Marjorie wearing a raincoat indoors? When I sit up, my body careens to the left, and then to the right, and it feels like the entire attic is on the back of a camel, swaying and swaying. The stillwaters clump in my throat like rotting leaves in a marsh, and I know—I *know*—the beast is down there, waiting. I rub the center of my chest.

Marjorie tilts the comic book to show me a drawing of Olive Oyl tumbling down a sand dune. I press a hand to my head. The pages ruffle, showing the inscription.

Love, Dad.

"Marjorie." My lips are so dry. "How did you *get* here?"

Marjorie didn't board the first trains out of Nottingham. Neither did I. We both stood in front of our house, watching the neighbors dragging heavy suitcases toward the station, their faces somber, their parents trying not to cry. The night before they left, my mother sat us down around the dining room table. "Many children are leaving the cities," she said. "Their parents believe it is safer in the country. But you must understand, girls, no place is safe anymore. Your father is not safe in Libya. Your uncle is not safe in London, working with the air chief marshal's offices. And so we will stay together, the three of us. We will do ourselves the work your father and the bakery boys did. We will look out for each other. Marjorie, you will take care of Emmaline, and Emmaline, you will take care of Marjorie."

She paused, and then gave my hand another squeeze. "But I will take care of you both a little extra, because I am your mother, and you will always be my two special rabbits."

Marjorie flips another page.

I can't stop coughing. I paw at the corner of the quilt, pressing it against my mouth, trying to hold in the stillwaters, but there is no stopping something like that.

Marjorie watches, and shakes her head sadly.

"Mother was right," she says. "No place is safe anymore."

34

IN MY DREAMS I hear Benny. *I know it was you, you thief.*
Marjorie comes and goes. She always wears her yellow raincoat. And then, suddenly, she is a black ghost with a white
face, only it isn't her at all anymore, but Sister Mary Grace
in her nun's habit.

She strokes my head.

"Shh," Sister Mary Grace says. "Try to rest, child."

There is someone else in the doorway. Muddy red hair
and a muddy red sweater.

"It's all right, Benedict," Sister Mary Grace says. "You
can go. She's waking up now."

He looks at me—wide eyes, no hint of his usual
sneer—and then quickly looks down and leaves through
the open door.

"He came and got me right away, and wouldn't leave until you woke. Now, try to drink some tea." Sister Mary Grace tips the edge of the steaming cup toward my lips.

I shake my head, trying to sit up. "I need to go outside. I need to visit the garden."

Her kindly look fades into consternation. "Not today, Emmaline."

How long have I been asleep and dreaming? Hours? *A whole day?* I throw a desperate look at the dark sky outside. I can just make out the garden wall in the moonlight. The moon, so bright it's blinding. Perfectly round. Full. *Full!* Panic starts to gnaw at the edges of my fingers, making them itch to pull on my boots and race downstairs.

"No," she says.

"Just for twenty minutes."

"No."

"Ten."

She gives me a look.

"Five!"

Sister Mary Grace sets down the cup with a sigh. "Dr. Turner examined you. Your body is very weak right now. You can't . . ." She looks down at the quilt. "You can't go outside. Not for a long time. I'm so sorry, my child." She looks over her shoulder at my door.

There is a new ticket there. *A red one.*

My blood thumps in my ears.

Not go outside?

Not go to the garden?

"You don't understand! Foxfire needs me. It's the full moon and the spectral shield isn't finished yet and the Black Horse might have already gotten to her!" I tear at the quilt, trying to get out of bed, but Sister Mary Grace holds me down. She's stronger than I remember, or else I am weaker.

"I'm so sorry. You must get some rest."

"I have to save her!"

"Em—"

"It's true! Everything Benny said is true! I did steal his comic book and I did steal the altar cloth and I'm sorry for all of it, but Foxfire needed it more than we did!" I swallow, try to speak more calmly. "If I don't go to her the Black Horse is going to kill her. *Tonight.*"

Sister Mary Grace looks like she is almost in tears. She stands, brushing at her eyes, and takes a deep, bolstering breath. "You've been talking nonsense in your sleep, and trying to get out." Her hand falls on a gleam of brass right above the knob. "Sister Constance had Thomas put a bolt on the door, for your own safety. We'll move you to Anna's room tomorrow. You'll be warmer there, and there's that pretty painted ceiling, won't you like that?"

I stare at the lock.

A bit of brass that wasn't there before holds me in now. Thomas must have come up with hammer and nails and turned my room into a prison cell. He knows about Foxfire. How could he do this to me?

I ball my fists in the quilt.

"Tell Thomas to come. Tell him I need to speak to him urgently. *Alone.*"

Sister Mary Grace hesitates. Other than to bring up firewood, Thomas rarely enters the upper levels in a house of nuns and young children. He almost never is alone with one of us, except for Anna, who was bedridden and needed extra help. Thomas is a young man, and even now, even in war, there are rules that must be followed.

Sister Mary Grace runs her finger over the lock, and then nods. "I'll tell him."

35

I SLEEP. I do not want to sleep, but it comes upon me as stealthy as a fox. I dream of my father and Thomas's father together on the Capuzzo front in armored cars. All around them, long black feathers rain down instead of bombs. Each feather slices at the car's armor, piece by piece by piece, letting in the snow.

Cold. It is so cold.

When I wake, the attic window is open a crack, which I do not remember doing. The thought of moving across the room to close it is too exhausting, so I just pull the quilt higher. My stomach rumbles, and I reach for the tea, and—

A letter rests beside the cup.

A letter on beautiful paper, rolled up in red ribbon.

My heart *flit-flit-flits*, just like the wounded bird that Marjorie found, as I pick it up with shaking fingers.

Dear Emmaline May,

As you know, my horses have been watching your world through the mirrors. They told me of your present condition as a prisoner, and I offer my condolences. In one of your letters, you expressed what—if I may presume—felt like deep anger toward the Black Horse. I fear this anger is misplaced. You see, the Black Horse does not bring strife because he enjoys it. He has a right to his life. He has a place in this world. He even has a name: Volkrig. My winged horses soar because that is what they do. Volkrig hunts because that is what he does. Try to understand. We can resist him. We can fight him. But we cannot blame him for doing what he was made to do.

Foxfire's fate is her own, now. You have been a good friend to her—and to me.

Ride true,
The Horse Lord

I fold the letter. *Volkrig.* The name has a sinister ring for a sinister horse, and yet, it changes something.

A chill slips from the cracked window.

The Horse Lord must have climbed through it. All this time, he could have just come to me. He didn't need the gardens, or the golden sundial. Why never show me his face?

Knock, knock.

The brass bolt draws back. "Emmaline? Are you awake?"

It is Thomas.

"Yes." I throw the covers back, but the stillwaters rise, and I cough and cough. Thomas looks in hesitantly, then quickly looks away.

"Sister Mary Grace said—"

"You must do me a favor." I force myself to sit up. "In Anna's bedroom. There's a desk with a secret drawer that's released by a latch in the bottom. There's a—" The stillwaters beast fights to claw up, and I swallow him back down. "There's a book. Take it to the sundial garden. Attach it to the ivy. You have to. Foxfire needs us."

He stares at me, as if not hearing. "Emmaline . . ."

"*Please!* I can't go myself."

He hesitates, and then nods. "Yes. Yes, of course I will."

I breathe out slowly, sinking into the pillows. They are soft. They are clouds, like Foxfire's hair.

But Thomas remains in the doorway. "There's something I have to tell you, Emmaline. My aunt's written from Wales. I have to leave later tonight, and I'll be gone for a few days. It's my father's funeral in London. It's poor timing," he stammers, glancing at the red ticket. "But there's nothing to be done for it."

He takes a deep breath, and then I understand. He thinks he will not see me again. He thinks the stillwaters will come for me while he is away. I snap my eyes to him.

"You think I'm going to die."

"No. No. I just . . ."

Yes. This is what he thinks.

His fingers toy with the brass bolt. "Goodbye, Emmaline." Then his hand drops to his pocket, and he takes out a small hand mirror. He sets it on my table next to the cold tea. It has brass edges and a wooden handle and I've no idea how he came by anything so fine.

There is a tag attached.

I hold it to the light.

For Emmaline May, from your friend Thomas.

"So the horses can look after you," he says. "While I'm gone."

36

IT IS DARK WHEN I WAKE.

Freezing rain pelts the cracked window. I barely remember sleeping. I so badly want to sleep again, but Thomas's visit has kindled my strength. I must know for certain that Foxfire is safe. I peel back the sweat-soaked sheets and climb shakily out of bed. My knees and ankles don't work properly, and the moment my feet touch down, I crumple to the floor, and crawl slowly to the window.

The clouds outside are heavy and mottled with full silver moonlight. I can just make out a fast shadow darting back and forth across the snow. Bog. Beside him trudges a looming, unbalanced shadow that must be Thomas. I hiss out a long breath of relief. Soon, at least, the spectral shield will be complete. Foxfire will be protected.

I scan the sky. Against the dark clouds—is that an even darker shadow? It flies in a tight circle, around and around, right over the hospital, just like a German plane.

Thunder cracks and I jump.

The Black Horse. Volkrig. Well, let him circle. He'll never find Foxfire now.

I ease the window closed and seal out the night with arms that feel so deeply weary.

The brass bolt slides back.

"Emmaline!" Sister Mary Grace hurries in. Sister Constance is right behind her. "What are you doing out of bed, child?"

I let my head tip forward to rest on the window's cool glass. Thunder cracks again, but I smile. Below, Thomas is opening the garden gate.

"Emmaline?" A cool hand presses against my forehead. I smell fresh, steaming tea. "Sister, help me get her into bed. She's burning up."

Those same cool hands lift me. Then, there are soft sheets. A bed that smells of straw. Pillows soft as clouds.

"It's so cold up here. We should bring her down to Anna's room right away. There's a fireplace."

But I like the smell up here, I want to say. *It reminds me of sheep, with their soft, soft wool.*

"But Dr. Turner said not to move her. He's coming back first thing in the morning."

"That might be too—"

"Shh." The hands are on my brow, pulling the sheets higher around my neck. "Emmaline? My child?"

"She can't hear you."

But I can. I can. I try to tell them, but only a ragged cough comes out. I taste something bitter. One of the nuns stifles a gasp, and then a cloth is pressed to my mouth.

I hear paper rustling.

"All these drawings. Do you think she . . . she really sees these horses in the mirrors?"

"Sister Mary Grace," Sister Constance chides. "It is our place to care for the children, not to indulge their feverish delusions." There are more hands around me, fluffing the pillow, and then Sister Constance adds softer, "Though part of me hopes that she does."

Sister Mary Grace still shuffles through my drawings. "If only there were someone to send them to. It's awful, isn't it? The reports of that bakery during the Nottingham blitz. The bombs, and then the fires. To lose your mother and sister like that—I can't imagine, and her father the same week in the siege of Tobruk." Her voice drops. "They were trapped, you know. Her mother and her sister. Dr. Turner heard it from the driver who brought her here. Emmaline was asleep in a different part of the bakery in the middle of the night—you know how she wanders off—when the bombs hit. She must have heard her family banging on the doors, but couldn't get to them in the rubble. She was burned badly."

My heart is *flit-flit-flit*ting.

No, I want to tell them. They're wrong. It wasn't my father. It wasn't my mother. It wasn't Marjorie—Marjorie was even here just yesterday, in her yellow raincoat! It was the horses, kicking at their stalls. The big bay gelding and two smaller mares. Spice. Ginger and Nutmeg.

Paper rustles again. "I suppose all the horses died too."

"Horses?" Sister Constance opens the door and shuts it behind them, but her voice still carries from the other side. "What horses? Her family worked at a bakery in the middle of Nottingham, far from the nearest pastures. She never had any horses."

The stillwaters are rising. They are rising and rising, drowning everything they touch. I can hear the horses kicking at their stalls. Their frightened yells sound almost like a person screaming. The stable door is shaking and shaking, but I can't get to it to let them out.

I can't help them.

I can't do anything at all.

When I open my eyes, I am alone, and the tea is long cold.

I release a fit of sobbing coughs. The stillwaters are rising fast now.

My head falls to the side. My reflection in Thomas's small hand mirror shows fever-red cheeks and damp tufts of hair. I snatch it up. Where are the winged horses? Why aren't they nosing through my tea on my bedside table? Why aren't they clomping against the wall behind me?

For Emmaline May, from your friend Thomas.

The handwriting is blocky and careful and somehow familiar. But ... no, it can't be Thomas's. Thomas can't write. It's tied to the mirror with ...

I sit abruptly.

No, no, no.

... It is tied with a silky red ribbon.

Outside, in the dark, there is a rumble of tires. Head-lights flash in the window. It must be Thomas's aunt come to take him away to London.

"No!" I throw back the sheets. No, the stillwaters haven't drowned me yet. No, Thomas hasn't left yet. No, no, no.

Benny can't be right.

The Horse Lord is real. He lives beyond the mirrors and he was friends with the old princess and he sent Foxfire to our world to protect her.

Thomas *can't* have written those letters.

37

THE HALLWAY CLOCK CHIMES. I lose count of the tolls but they go on for a while—it's getting late. I make my way slowly down the residence hallway, leaning against the wall for support. All the doors are closed. The soft sounds of sleeping children seep through the cracks in the doors. On the walls, the mirrors are empty. No winged horses watch my journey.

I pass a window and push back the wool blanket. Outside, in the lights of a car, a woman in a brown coat is talking to Sister Constance. It is snowing harder now, and the car's windshield wipers are fighting a losing battle. I can no longer see the moon overhead, but it is there, shining full silver light over everything. Sister Mary Grace holds a piece of rope attached to Bog's collar so that he won't run off after his master when the car leaves.

Thomas emerges from his cottage with a small, plain suitcase.

I press a hand against the frosted glass. "Not yet!" I cry. But my voice doesn't carry. I lurch down the hall, into the library with Mr. Mason's Christmas tree still in the corner. I fumble with the latch on the window until it pushes open. Wind and snow howl at me, but I howl right back. Fingers clawing at the window frame, I manage to get one leg through.

"Thomas!"

He doesn't hear over the wind.

"Thomas, don't go!"

My other foot catches on the icy windowsill; I slip and tumble into the bush. Bog jumps up and starts barking, and I hear someone cry out, and then the car's headlights are pointing toward me and I shield my eyes, the snow blowing harder, and squint into the light.

Bog runs up, the rope dangling from his collar, and licks my face. A second later a shadow looms over me. Thomas. He wraps his coat around my shoulders, then picks me up with his one arm, just like he did the lamb that day. His arm doesn't shake at all.

"Emmaline, what are you doing out here?" He's already carrying me toward the warmth of the house. He shouts to the woman in the car. "Five minutes!"

He hurries us up the steps as the snow stings our faces, shoulders open the door, sets me down on the princess's sofa by the Christmas tree, and tugs down one of the wool blankets to tuck around me. "Hang on. Let me fetch Sister Mary—"

"No!" I claw into his arm. With my other hand I dig out the tag. It is damp with sweat and crumpled, and I hold it up like an accusation. "It's you, isn't it?" I yell. "It was you all along! I should have listened to Benny. *You* wrote the letters!"

A light flickers in the doorway. Sister Constance, coming in from outside, holding a lantern.

Thomas's eyes go wide.

"You said you couldn't read or write!" I accuse.

He shakes his head, holding out his hand like I am something that might shatter at any moment. "I didn't say that. You misunderstood."

"*You* wrote the letters!"

"No, please—"

"Tell the truth!"

"All right!" His voice is strained. "What do you want me to say? I lied to you! Is that what you want to hear? I did write the letters."

I stare at him. No, no, it isn't possible.

But maybe I have been keeping too many secrets, even from myself.

Maybe Marjorie and her yellow raincoat are gone.

Maybe Mama and Papa are gone.

Maybe the bakery and our home are gone too. And maybe the stillwaters—the *tuberculosis*—is just as bad as Dr. Turner says it is. I start to breathe very fast. Am I ... am I going to die here? Like Anna? Like Mama, and Papa, and Marjorie? And I press a hand to my chest, but there's no breath there. I am empty.

"There is no Horse Lord," I sob. "You made it all up. You never saw the winged horses in the mirrors."

His eyes go wide. "I wasn't lying about that. I saw them. I swear."

"Liar!"

The left side of his face crinkles as if he doesn't know what to do. His hand runs over his mouth, kneading at the skin and the bridge of his nose. "I'm not a liar." He glances over his shoulder at Sister Constance. He turns back to me, and his eyes are determined. His mouth is set firmly. "There's something I haven't told you. I did write those letters, yes, but I didn't make it up." He sets his hand over mine. "Emmaline. *I* am the Horse Lord."

I stop crying. The clock is *tick-tick-tick*ing in the hallway. Behind us, Sister Constance's lantern is flickering.

Thomas's eyes are so green. Thomas, the Horse Lord? Thomas, who shovels turnips and throws sticks for an old collie—the Horse Lord? Thomas, the monster in all of Benny's stories—the Horse Lord?

Over his shoulder, the mirror above the fireplace is still empty.

"I don't believe you." I am shaking my head, shaking and shaking and shaking some more. "You're still lying. There is no Horse Lord. There are no winged horses, and there never were!"

His face flickers. Sister Constance has one hand pressed to her mouth, and the lantern is shaking in the other. A sulfur-tasting bubble rises up my throat. The stillwaters, fighting back.

Thomas cradles his face in his hand, shaking his head too, and then suddenly he looks up. His eyes aren't sad anymore. "I can prove it! Wait here."

He pushes up from the floor and runs past Sister Constance down the hall. His boots echo in the long corridor. So does the sound of the kitchen door slamming shut. Bog starts barking from outside. The snow is coming down harder now. The car is still running, its engine clunking outside as the windshield wipers go back and forth, back and forth.

Can I tell you a secret?

I want to believe Thomas.

I want to believe he is the Horse Lord. I want to believe that Foxfire is safe in the sundial garden and that Anna has a set of wings now and that the winged horses still live in the mirrors and that Volkrig, sinister Volkrig, will forever be prevented from landing on this protected place.

The kitchen door slams again. Thomas comes running down the hall, snow caught in his hair and eyelashes and the shoulders of his coat. He gets to one knee and holds out a wooden box.

It is beautiful, this box. It gleams with polish. There is an insignia carved into the top, a regal-looking crest that couldn't belong to anyone other than a king or a prince—or a lord.

Thomas opens it and hands me a shiny silver medal on a crisp red ribbon.

I run my fingers over it slowly as my eyes go wide.

On it is a majestic horse rising on two legs. Two wings stretch out from its shoulders as it takes flight. A rider sits on its back in a magnificent crown and cape.

My mouth drops open.

"You mean . . ."

"These are precious treasures from my land beyond the mirrors," he says. "I brought them with me when I crossed over."

My eyes go even wider as I look at the treasure. They look like soldiers' medals, but these are different. Special. I can just *tell.* Many have horses on them. Some with wings, some without. Some with riders, some on their own. The horses' magnificent metal muscles tear across unseen wind. Each ribbon is a different color of the rainbow: purple, and red, and blue as deep as the sea.

And there is more treasure too. There's a gold ring that seems almost too big for Thomas, a pair of emerald jewels, and a golden pocket watch. Everything gleams in polished silvers and golds, more valuable than anything I've ever seen in my life. In the lamplight, the Horse Lord's treasure shimmers.

Is it true?

Is everything he has said true?

Thomas closes the box. Words are carved into the wooden top around the royal insignia:

Utrinque Paratus. Bellerophon et Pegasus.

It must be the language of the world beyond the mirror.

"Do you believe me now?" Thomas whispers.

I press a hand to my mouth. I want to hold in the still-waters. I want to hold in my voice. I want to hold in everything, but tears come out anyway. "But . . . why didn't you tell me?"

Outside, the car honks. He throws a look over his shoulder.

"I should have," he says quickly. I never noticed before, but the way his hair curls really isn't like a wild bear at all, but like it is made for a crown to rest upon it. "But it was a secret. I'm not supposed to live in this world. I didn't have a choice, though, you see? I'm like Foxfire. Wounded. But for me, what's broken is on the inside. I've been running from the Black Horse too, all this time. You've been protecting us both."

My mouth drops open.

"These are precious treasures from my land beyond the mirrors."

He reaches out and touches my cheek. Outside, the car honks again, and I remember that his father has died. The funeral in London.

Did his father know who he truly was?

"I must go." He closes the box and stands. "Thank you, Emmaline. And . . . ride true."

He takes the treasure from his world with him. As he slips down the hall, the last thing I see is the royal insignia carved on the front of the box, flashing in the lamplight.

Sister Constance presses a hand to her chest. She is fighting tears.

"Come along, child." She has to clear her throat. "Time for bed. Into Anna's room. Sister Mary Grace has a fire going."

A fire? But why do I need a fire? I am ablaze inside. There is no way the snow and the cold can reach me now. And then I realize that maybe Papa and Mama and Marjorie aren't gone at all—maybe they're just in the world beyond the mirror, with Anna and the Horse Lord's father, stretching their wings, hooves prancing in the sun.

Sister Constance rests one hand on my shoulder, and then presses it against my forehead.

I am ablaze.

38

HOW STRANGE TO BE in Anna's room without Anna. The blanket isn't as warm. There is no smell of lavender anymore.

After Sister Constance pours medicine down my throat, she feels my forehead, and sighs. Her eyes go to Christ on the crucifix hanging above the bed. She makes the sign of the cross. Then her eyes go to the floating gods on the ceiling, and I can't believe it—she whispers a prayer to them, too.

"Ring this." She presses a bell into my hand. "If you need me. Dr. Turner will be here first thing in the morning."

As soon as she is gone, I roll over toward Anna's desk with the secret drawer. Even broken, maybe one of the colored pencils' tips is still good, and I can draw the Horse

Lord's winged horse-and-rider insignia before I forget what it looks like. My fingers fumble to pull the latch, and the secret drawer pops open. There is the box of pencils, just where I put them, broken bits rattling. And the paper. And . . .

My hand stills.

No.

No, this can't be right.

Beneath the papers, right where I hid it, Popeye looks back at me. Benny's comic book. My heart drums in my chest, threatening to stir the stillwaters. But Thomas promised. I saw his shadow outside with Bog. . . .

Then I see that Anna's naturalist book with the dog-eared pages is gone, and I understand: Thomas kept his promise—but *he took the wrong book.*

Outside, the wind groans. Small cracks in the windowsill let in slips of cold that ruffle the heavy blanket. The corner is still pinned up. Beyond the windows, there is a blustering wall of snow. And then something flickers in the bright moonlight, and I gasp.

A black shadow.

I throw off the covers and scramble to the other window, but the car is gone. Thomas is gone. I start for the door but my legs won't hold me up. I sink to the sooty old rug, coughing at the dust.

Volkrig is out there, and it's a full moon, and he can see everything, he can see Foxfire!

I twist toward the bell—I'll ring for Sister Constance—but no, she will only put me back in bed. I could crawl down the hall—the three little mice's room is next door to Anna's—but I have told them before about the winged horses. They don't believe me.

I clutch the comic book tightly, tightly, as tight as my lungs feel now, and then I twist toward the door.

There is no one left to save her but me.

I wrap Anna's coat around me and put on her slippers with shaking hands. I shove the comic book in the large inside breast pocket and hug it to my chest. And I think of Foxfire out there alone. She must be so scared.

What if I'm already too late?

My hand slides off the doorknob. I'm sweating too much, but I eventually get out and down the hall and through the front door. Snow stings my face all the way down to my scalp. I draw the coat tighter and slip out in the snow. It's gotten deeper in just a few hours.

The night is so dark, I can see only a few feet from the hospital: snow, and night, and my own blowing tufts of hair. The sundial garden might as well be in Berlin.

I crawl through snow that soaks into my nightgown. My socks, my shirt, Anna's coat are all cold and wet, and I can't keep from shivering. I crawl. My fingers are red at the tips. I didn't know cold could burn before now. I keep crawling through the trenches of snow. My face feels too tight in the cold, and I've lost feeling in my nose. Bullets of ice assault me. But I keep crawling, until a wall of ivy looms in the darkness. With aching bare fingers I take hold of the twisting vines. I pull myself up. I climb. And climb. The wind tries to push me back down. The ivy wraps around my bare ankles, but I kick it away, and throw a leg over the top. And then my legs give out, and the stillwaters come and I am falling, and falling, and falling.

39

SOMETHING WARM NUZZLES MY NOSE.

I blink. The sky is filled with thousands of shooting stars, moving back and forth like will-o'-the-wisps, like the tiny glowing creatures Anna told me about, too many to wish on at once. I'm asleep in a cloud that is soft, so soft, that I could lie here forever.

And then a warm gray muzzle and deep brown eyes and a blaze in the shape of a spark push themselves into my vision.

"Foxfire!"

I sit up in a snowdrift, amid the churning flakes that aren't shooting stars at all, and throw my arms around her neck. She smells of apples. I stroke her with shaking fingers, crying because she is still here.

"I was so afraid." I pull back, searching her eyes. "I—"

A shadow passes overhead, and we both look up.

A dark stain moves across the clouds, impossibly high, in precise circles. I catch my breath, holding it tight. My fingers knit against Foxfire's muzzle as both our eyes follow the shadow.

Volkrig's black wings beat once, and then he veers sharply toward us. His circles spiral tighter and tighter, until he is just over the sundial garden.

"He's seen us!"

I grapple for the comic book and collapse to my knees. Foxfire noses me around the neck, around my back, as though searching for a wound, but she'll never find it in any of those places. My wounds run deeper.

Volkrig's shadow passes over us.

And then, Foxfire lets out a snort. For a painful second, I think one of Volkrig's sharp black feathers has sliced her just like in my dream about Papa. But no. Her eyes are alert, her ears swiveled forward. Her head lowers first and then one knobby knee, and then the other, and then her rump rolls down to the snow too. She looks over her shoulder at me.

I gasp.

If I cannot walk, then she will carry me.

With numb fingers I grab ahold of the base of her mane. I use my last bit of strength to pull myself up until I'm lying half on her back. She stands slowly, one jerky movement at a time.

"To the far wall," I whisper. "To the spectral shield."

She moves in quick steps, as aware as I am of Volkrig circling above. A sudden shriek tears the night. No hawk is that loud. No owl is that full of rage. And then the pressure in the air changes. The snow is suddenly blowing in the wrong direction, away from us. In its place, black feathers rain down. Dozens of them, the length of my arm and sharp as blades. I cry out as one slices against my skin.

When I look up, Volkrig is ten feet above us.

"No!"

I am so close. The protective shield is almost complete. As Foxfire nears the wall I stretch out as far as I can, the comic book clutched in my hand. Almost. I am five inches away. Three. So close—

Foxfire lets out a cry as a black feather slices her. Her haunches bunch, and I know that any moment she is going to bolt. But the gate is closed. There is no place to run this time.

I stretch farther. One inch away!

But then the shadow lowers. The sound of his wings is deafening. One midnight-black hoof the size of my head kicks at my arm and I scream. The comic book falls facedown. *Orange side down.*

No!

I lean over as far as I can, but there's no way I can reach it. Volkrig kicks his hooves again, and all I can smell is rot, as thick as putrid seaweed. Another shriek tears the sky.

There is no place to run.

Foxfire rears. I cry out, squeezing my legs as hard as I can to keep from falling off. The beating, beating, beating of Volkrig's twenty-foot wings churn the snow around us. When I dare to look up, midnight hooves as sharp as knives and as strong as bludgeons paw the air. Nostrils rimmed in red flare.

But his eyes. His eyes are not cruel.

He has his place, I think. *This is what he does.* Foxfire's muscles bunch beneath me, and my heart clenches. Maybe it isn't his fault. Maybe he can't be blamed. But this is what *we* do— we fight. And we will continue to fight until we can fight no longer.

"Go!" I cry.

Foxfire needs no more encouragement. I dig my bare ankles into her sides to hold on as she runs. She races amid the maze of gardens, her hooves throwing up snow behind us. Volkrig's shadow follows. Foxfire turns sharply into the herb garden, and then the statuary. Each gate is sealed. Each wall too high to jump. The shadow follows. Sea and rot, right on top of us. His wings beat harder. His midnight hooves gnash at our backs. My nightgown rips, and I feel the sting of torn skin on my shoulder, but I don't let go of Foxfire's mane.

There has to be a way out of the gardens.

There has to.

This is what *I* do. I do not give in.

I dig my heels into her sides, and Foxfire weaves around a stone pond with a statue of Apollo. A crash sounds behind us. Volkrig's hooves have slammed into it and broken off Apollo's head. We reach the end of the garden and I guide Foxfire to the right, into the rose garden. It's narrower here. Overgrown. Scraggly briars catch at us, but at least the domed branches slow Volkrig. The tunnel of winter-dead roses ends and we are spit out into a sudden wide expanse. Skeletons of azaleas flank the sides, but there is nothing overhead. No trellises. No overgrown vines.

Only snow and a sinister shadow.

Fear plunges deep in my chest. Is this how it ends?

But Foxfire doesn't stop running. I dig in my heels, nudging her to the left to circle back around to the sundial garden, but she ignores me. Her head is down, and her mane is whipping in my face, and her muscles are ice and steel. And then something rumbles beneath my knees.

I gasp.

She paws the earth one more time, and then leaps into the night. Twenty-foot wings sweep out on either side. I clutch her mane, wrapping my ankles tighter, as my heart stops with the thrill. Healed! At last, she is healed! Wind races by us. It tangles in my hair and it pushes at her wings and it lifts us.

We

are

flying.

We are flying.

40

I FORGET ABOUT VOLKRIG. I forget about the still-waters and the freezing wind.

Foxfire's body is so alive beneath me. Her white wings beat with the sound of thunder. Her shoulders ripple as she lunges for clouds, each one higher than the next.

Dizzy, I look down to see the map of the overgrown garden beneath us. We fly above the barren rosebushes with their sharp briars. Above the broken fountain and hungry ivy. We fly above the hospital roof. We fly above the spectral shield that, without the comic book, shall never be quite finished, but that is okay. We are our own prism of light now.

I press a hand to my chest, but up here, the air is so clear that I don't feel the urge to cough. I can pull air into my lungs, and there are no murky stillwaters, not one drip. The next time I look down, we fly even above Volkrig.

The Black Horse is nothing but a memory.

Foxfire beats her wings, and takes us even higher. I want to go high, high, as high as the sky.

41

I WONDER IF MARJORIE'S bird with the broken wings ever made it this high.

I wonder if any living creature at all ever makes it this high, or if it is only the realm for floating gods.

42

CAN I TELL YOU A SECRET?

I know now why the Horse Lord crossed into our world and called himself Thomas and lived in a little cottage. It is because our world that stretches out below—the hills and the trees and the sun breaking over the rooftops—is more than just brown and gray. There is color there. There are greens and reds and blues as deep as the sea.

You just have to know where to look.

43

WHEN I WAKE, I am staring at white clouds.

It takes a moment to recognize the painting on the ceiling of Anna's room. My head aches in a dull way, and my throat is very dry, but I feel warm.

I sit up.

The windows are open, and fresh air drifts in. A tray of steaming tea sits on the bedside table. The silver bell to ring for the Sisters. A brand-new bottle filled with syrupy yellow medicine. Dr. Turner must have come.

Little Arthur is sitting at the foot of my bed, drawing quietly, bent over a fan of loose pages. Anna's broken pencils are scattered on the quilt, and he is trying to draw with the broken nub of the blue pencil.

I look out the window. How many days have I been

here, recovering? The last thing I remember is Foxfire's wings beating the air as the sun rose above the horizon, casting the sky in shades of pinks and purples. And the sun was so beautiful, a soft yellow, the same yellow as the butter that is melting on a piece of toast next to the tea.

Toast.

I'm famished.

I draw in a deep breath, hesitantly testing my lungs. I take a bite, and the toast slips down my sore throat. That clawing pain has lessened. I feel better.

I whirl to look at my open door.

The red ticket is gone.

I spin toward Arthur. "What happened?" From the way my body aches, I must have fallen off of Foxfire and tumbled down to earth. "Did the Sisters find me in a snow-drift?"

But Arthur never speaks, and he does not speak now.

A strange worry creeps into my stomach and I whirl toward the side mirror. It is empty. I pick up the hand mirror that Thomas gave me—empty too. And so is the one above the dresser. I grab up the teaspoon and stare into it at my misshapen reflection.

Nothing.

Where are the winged horses?

Where have they gone?

I roll over and paper rumples. I pull out a wad of messy

pages that someone has left beside me. The Popeye comic book! The last I saw, it had fallen in the snow. It is warped and dirty, but someone must have found it and tried to smooth out the pages. There is a note attached in Benny's writing.

I'm sorry I broke your pencils. I'm glad you're getting well. I forgive you for stealing my comic book. You may borrow it, if you like.

Sincerely,
Benny

(P.S.—but only until you feel better!)

I stare at the inscription.

Benny has shared his dearest object with me.

Have I floated into a different world, a gentler one? I look around in a daze, but the same gods still float on the ceiling, the same wool blanket is pinned back by the window.

And then Arthur sighs at the broken blue pencil that won't draw, and I realize that I have done something magical. I have been to the heavens on the back of a winged horse—I am a real explorer, just like Anna said I was.

An idea strikes me. I take out Anna's sewing knife from the secret drawer, and the closest pencil, the orange one.

It is snapped in two, the point broken. I press the blade against one of the halves and shave. I shave until it is sharpened into a point as fine as Anna kept them, and then I sharpen the other half, too.

Now there are two orange pencils.

I hand one to Arthur.

"You may borrow this, if you like," I say.

Arthur blinks a few times, and then takes it and dives back into his pages, drawing faster now. In a flurry, I snatch up the other broken pieces of pencils. I sharpen the point of 868-LAPIS BLUE, and the broken shards of 876-HELIOTROPE PURPLE, until all the broken pencils are whole again. Now there are enough for Arthur and me and all the children in the hospital to have their own pieces of color.

And then I look closer at Arthur's drawing. It is rough and childlike. The back legs are bent the wrong way, but the wings . . .

"Can I see that, Arthur?"

He hands me the paper, and glances at the mirror on Anna's wall, and then immediately starts in on another. There is a flicker of movement to my left, where I have placed the mirror that Thomas gave me.

I whip my head in its direction, and she is there.

Foxfire.

She stands quietly to the side of the mirror-bed, gazing a little wistfully out the mirror-window, where the blanket

"Arthur," I say slowly, "do you see those horses in the mirror?"

is pinned back to let in light. There are traces of my tea on her muzzle.

"Foxfire!"

She turns. She has heard me. For once, my voice has carried through the mirror, and she blinks her soft brown eyes at me.

Another horse joins her. It is brown and delicate and smells like lavender. I can just tell. And next to her—next to her are a gelding and two mares. Sandy with dark manes.

"I knew you'd come back," I tell them.

Arthur has turned to face the mirror too. I peer closer at the paper in my hand. The horse in his drawing is white with a gray muzzle. Between her eyes is a blaze in the shape of a spark.

My heart goes *rat-a-tat, rat-a-tat.*

I think of how Arthur is always gazing at reflective things—the kitchen ladle, the tin washtub, the Christmas ornaments—and realize maybe it isn't just Thomas and me who see the horses.

"Arthur," I say slowly, "do you see those horses in the mirror?"

But Arthur says nothing.

"You see them, don't you?"

And again, Arthur says nothing.

But slowly, a smile spreads between his pink, pink cheeks.

AUTHOR'S NOTE

The first glimmer of an idea for *The Secret Horses of Briar Hill* came to me during a long drive to a librarian's conference across my home state of North Carolina. My car radio was broken, and I found myself alone with a rare few hours of silence. As I drove past farms and horses, my mind wandered, and I thought about all the books that had deeply affected me as a child. I devoured books like *The Secret Garden* and the Chronicles of Narnia, which combined reality with dreams, history with fantasy, darkness with heart, and, most of all, contained true magic. I started to daydream about a magical place, and by the time I arrived at my destination, Emmaline felt as real to me as a sister.

I began to work on this book by looking into childhood illnesses and World War II, and my research took a sudden personal turn. My grandfather passed away a few years ago, and while working on *The Secret Horses of Briar Hill*, I happened to find a collection of paperwork and memorabilia from his time serving in the U.S. Army Air Forces during World War II. When he was only eighteen, his plane was shot down over Italy, and he was put into a German prisoner-of-war camp, from which he was fortunately freed a year later. The grim man in the black-and-white prisoner-of-war photo I discovered contrasted greatly with the warm, loving man I had known. My grandfather had run a farm and raised a family. He loved fishing, and regularly indulged in homemade apple pie. Among his things was a letter he'd written about the importance of finding beauty in the darkness of war, and this left a deep impact on me. I decided to convey this sense in my story through the eyes of someone small and alone, who had that rare ability to find such beauty.

In order to capture the atmosphere of wartime Britain, where Emmaline lived, I turned to the BBC's WWII People's War project, a wealth of firsthand accounts from soldiers, nurses, civilians, and children who lived through this period. I read about a doctor who created a color-coded diagnosis system for children with tuberculosis, much like Dr. Turner does. I read about a nurse who fell in love with a soldier so ill that he could never be kissed—just like Anna. And as I researched tuberculosis, I thought about how for children, illness could be parallel to the battles adult soldiers were fighting.

You might be curious to know what other parts of this book are based on historical fact. Though Briar Hill hospital is fictional, there were several children's hospitals and tuberculosis wards operating during the war. Occasionally parents were allowed to visit their children, though they were often separated by glass partitions to prevent the spread of disease. Because of the crowded conditions and limited resources, tuberculosis was more prevalent during the war years, but due to medical advancements, by 1945 cases of tuberculosis were in decline (with a sharp drop in the 1950s after vaccines were developed). Today, though tuberculosis has been nearly eradicated in the United States and Great Britain, one-third of the world's population is infected with this disease.

Emmaline called tuberculosis the *stillwaters* after the Latin proverb "still waters run deep," which means that quiet people are often hiding a deeper nature. To Emmaline, this saying meant that children may be overlooked as being simple, but they are often struggling with deeper battles, such as illnesses, that aren't always visible on the surface.

When Emmaline describes her neighbors leaving the major cities for the safety of the country, she is talking about Operation Pied Piper, part of a greater evacuation in Great Britain during which over 3.5 million people were relocated. Shropshire, the region where Briar Hill hospital is located, was a prime destination for children, as it was far from major cities or factories that might have been a target for bombings. Emmaline's family's bakery was inspired by a real building, the Co-op Bakery, located on Meadow Lane in Nottingham, which was badly bombed during the Nottingham Blitz in May of 1941.

Thomas's father, Sergeant Whatley, is fictitious, though inspired by true commanders such as Lieutenant General Frederick Browning, Major-General John Campbell, and Lieutenant General William Gott. The emblems on Thomas's father's war medal, along with the sayings *Utrinque Paratus* and *Bellerophon et Pegasus,* are real. The medal comes from the British First Airborne division and was also used by soldiers trained in the Special Air Services; its insignia of a winged horse and rider was rumored to have been designed by Browning's wife, the celebrated author Daphne du Maurier (whose books happen to be among my favorites).

Many readers ask me what exactly happened to Emmaline in this story. Some think she didn't survive her illness, and the final chapters represent her dream of being at peace. Some believe she did survive and stayed at Briar Hill to help the other children. I do not think there is an answer, just as I cannot tell you if Thomas really is the Horse Lord, or if the winged horses were real or existed only in Emmaline's imagination. I think each reader is entitled to believe what she or he wants to believe. Whatever Emmaline's truth, I know for certain that darkness can be defeated by hope, and I know that one girl, no matter how small, can make her dreams come alive.

Ride true,
Megan Shepherd

ACKNOWLEDGMENTS

It is fitting that the idea for Emmaline's story came to me on a road trip, because creating this book was its own journey, and I'm fortunate to have worked with such a special cast of real-life characters along the way.

I knew Rebecca Weston was the perfect editor for this book when she sent me her own spectral shield complete with eight magical colored objects. As we worked together, I was deeply inspired by her dedication to craft, her keen insight, and her passion for timeless storytelling. In short, Rebecca, you made me believe in magic again.

My agent, Josh Adams at Adams Literary, championed this book right from the start. His belief in this story gave me confidence at a time I desperately needed it, and I am grateful for his unwavering support. Also, I am especially grateful to A. Adams, this book's first young reader, for her advice and enthusiasm.

Thank you to my early readers, Megan Miranda, Carrie Ryan, and April Tucholke, who were kind enough to offer critiques and invaluable friendship. Thank you as well to my friend James Ballantine for lending his expertise on British military history, and to my father-in-law, Gene Shepherd, for his medical knowledge.

I'd like to express my gratitude to the team at Delacorte Press and Random House, who have also championed this book: Barbara Marcus, Beverly Horowitz, Judith Haut, Dominique Cimina, Anna Gjesteby, John Adamo, Kim Lauber, Melissa Zar, Nick Elliot, Laura Antonacci, Adrienne Waintraub, Lisa Nadel, Kate Gartner, Heather Kelly, Jenica Nasworthy, Colleen Fellingham, Tamar Schwartz, Alice Rahaeuser, Shameiza Ally, Susan Hecht, Kate Sullivan, and Whitney Conyers. Also a special thank you to Daniel Burgess for creating such striking artwork.

And finally, my husband, Jesse, can be blamed for encouraging me to stare at walls and daydream in the first place. Thank you for believing in me.

And as always, a special thanks to my readers. If writing this book was a journey, then you are the destination, and I hope my words have found a home in your hearts.

ABOUT THE AUTHOR

MEGAN SHEPHERD grew up in her family's independent bookstore in the Blue Ridge Mountains. She is the author of several acclaimed young adult books, and *The Secret Horses of Briar Hill* is her debut middle-grade novel. Shepherd now lives and writes on a 125-year-old farm outside Asheville, North Carolina, with her husband, two cats, and a dog. You can visit her at meganshepherd.com.